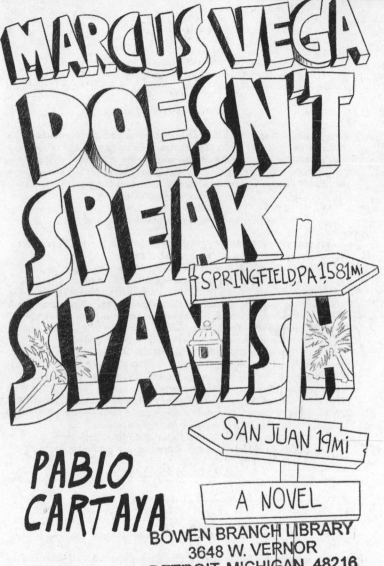

MARCUS VEGA DOESN'T SPEAK SPANISH

SPRINGFIELD, PA 1,581 Mi

SAN JUAN 19 Mi

PABLO CARTAYA

A NOVEL

PUFFIN BOOKS

PUFFIN BOOKS
An imprint of Penguin Random House LLC, New York

First published in the United States of America by Viking,
an imprint of Penguin Random House LLC, 2018
Published by Puffin Books, an imprint of Penguin Random House LLC, 2019

Visit us online at penguinrandomhouse.com

THE LIBRARY OF CONGRESS HAS CATALOGED THE VIKING EDITION AS FOLLOWS:
Names: Cartaya, Pablo, author.
Title: Marcus Vega doesn't speak Spanish / by Pablo Cartaya.
Other titles: Marcus Vega does not speak Spanish
Description: New York : Viking, [2018] | Summary: After a fight at school leaves
Marcus facing suspension, Marcus's mother takes him and his younger brother,
who has Down syndrome, to Puerto Rico to visit relatives they do not remember or
have never met, and while there Marcus starts searching for his father, who left
their family ten years ago and is somewhere on the island.
Identifiers: LCCN 2017052895 | ISBN 9781101997260 (hardcover)
Subjects: | CYAC: Families—Fiction. | Puerto Ricans—United States—Fiction.|
Down syndrome—Fiction. | People with mental disabilities—Fiction. | Middle
schools—Fiction. | Schools—Fiction. | Puerto Rico—Fiction. | BISAC: JUVENILE
FICTION / People & Places / United States / Hispanic &Latino. | JUVENILE
FICTION / Family / General (see also headings under Social Issues). | JUVENILE
FICTION / Social Issues / Special Needs.
Classification: LCC PZ7.C24253 Mar 2018 | DDC [Fic]—dc23
LC record available at https://lccn.loc.gov/2017052895

Puffin Books ISBN 9781101997284

Design by Kate Renner
Text set in Velo Serif

Printed in the United States of America

3 5 7 9 10 8 6 4 2

A la gente de Puerto Rico,

This story is for you . . . Pa'lante siempre.

MISUNDERSTAND

verb: to fail to understand (someone or something) correctly

FAMILY

noun: any of various social units differing from but regarded as equivalent to the traditional family

*"The monsters of our childhood
do not fade away,
neither are they ever
wholly monstrous."*

—John le Carré

ONE

MONSTER BUSINESS

Most kids clear out of the way when I walk down the hall. They're like campers in a forest who spot a grizzly and scramble up a tree to hide. (Or, in this case, climb into a locker.) I've been called the Mastodon of Montgomery Middle, the Springfield Skyscraper, the Moving Mountain, the Terrible Tower, the . . . You get the idea.

These names bothered me in sixth grade when I was excited to start middle school and make friends. But now, in eighth grade, my size has become a profit center. And business is booming.

Take these two kids sitting down in the back corner of the library (my office), fidgeting like I'm going to eat them or something. One has practically chewed off his fingernails, and the other one's leg won't stop bouncing.

I hear them whispering.

"What?" I say.

"Is it true?" the kid asks. "That you carried forty-two chairs to the auditorium? By yourself?"

I stare. "Yes."

Actually it was only eight chairs, but these are the kinds of rumors that are good for business.

"Incredible."

They start whispering to each other again.

"We're wondering if we could procure your walking services, Mr. Marcus?"

"Don't call me that."

At the start of the school year, a bunch of sixth graders confused me for a teacher while they were trying to find the auditorium. I told them they'd better figure out where they needed to go or I was going to collect a tax from them for getting in the way. They ran. Soon a rumor started spreading that I was really an undercover assistant principal hired to keep kids in line. It's kind of ridiculous, but things at Montgomery often are.

The rumors about me have gone from fantastical (Godzilla with a crew cut) to realistic (assistant principal). It's really annoying. But like I said, I've found a way to make it work for me. These two kids are here for my walking service, the crown jewel of my business.

"Five bucks a week to walk each of you to school," I say. "And five bucks to get you home. Your total invoice is ten per week."

"Each of us?" The kid seems surprised.

"I could walk you halfway for half the price."

They look at each other a moment.

"That's my blue-plate special," I say.

"No, we'll take the whole service. Thank you."

"Where do you live?"

"I live on Maple and Vine," one kid says.

The other kid chimes in with, "I'm on Vine and North Cherry Hill Drive."

I already walk four other kids who live in the Cherry Hill neighborhood, so two more isn't a big deal. I can't charge them more than ten bucks, or parents will start to wonder. The way I see it, it's a win-win for everyone. I'm making some money, and these kids are getting protection from bullying on their walks to and from school. I'm doing a service. People pay for bodyguards all the time. That's what I am to these kids—a big, bad bodyguard.

"Hey," I tell them before they run off to class. "There's a deposit. Five bucks each."

I always take a deposit for my services. It's like

insurance money. They both pull out fives and hand them to me. Then they quickly get out of my office.

Most of my business transactions happen in the small cubicle located behind a shelf at the far end of the library. The school librarian lets me hang there whenever I want. I usually take a stack of books to read while I wait for my "clients." In exchange for the office space, I help the librarian shelve books.

I carefully fold the cash into my pocket and pull out my business spiral from my backpack to write down the names of my new clients. I check my CELL PHONE STORAGE tab before I close it. I need to pick up the slack on that. I've only collected two cell phones today. That's just three bucks.

Here at Montgomery, there is zero cell phone use during school hours. Kids were getting their phones stolen and/or thrown into the lunchtime garbage can by older kids. (Trust me, you don't want your cell phone tossed in there. I don't even put my own garbage in there.) Besides all of that, Principal Jenkins said students were "spending too much time texting and using social media."

Some parents cheered Principal Jenkins's decision. Others, not so much. In the end, a compromise was made. Kids could have a phone in their lockers but were not permitted to carry them around, and they definitely could not have them in class.

Around mid-September, two seventh graders bumped into me because they were texting each other while walking to class. They tried to apologize, but I saw an opportunity. I decided to take their phones and charge them a "storage fee" until school got out. I let them come to my locker, send a text or two, then return the phones until they left school. I've collected phones one hundred and twenty-seven times since school started. That's almost two hundred bucks.

I look at another tab in my portfolio.

GARBAGE TAX COLLECTION (YEAR TWO)
WEEK 25 = $2

Business is way down. I started collecting a garbage tax last year when kids kept dumping stuff on the floor, leaving empty soda cans in the library or crumpled paper in classrooms. It became so bad, Principal Jenkins said he would give detention to any student caught littering on school grounds. That's how the garbage tax was born.

The idea came to me when I was sitting in my office and I heard a couple of kids chatting. I stood and peeked over the shelves to find a boy and girl had sneaked two sodas into the library. They finished, left the cans on a shelf, and took a few books to the circulation desk.

I walked over, grabbed the evidence, and waited for them outside.

The girl was surprised to see me standing there. She stepped back and tried to smile. "Hi," she said.

I showed them the cans. "Know what this means?" I asked.

The girl looked worried. "Please don't tell," she said. "My parents will kill me if I get detention."

"We can pay you!" the boy blurted out.

"How much?" I said.

"Um . . ." The boy looked at the girl.

"Twenty-five cents," the girl offered.

"Fifty," I said.

They looked at each other again.

"Fifty cents to save our butts from detention?"

"How do we know you won't tell?" the girl asked.

"Because I would have already told if I didn't think there was something I could get out of it."

"Fair enough," the girl said. "Here you go." She shook my hand and gave me a dollar. "For me and my friend."

I took the money and threw the cans into the recycling bin. I wrote in my spiral the date I collected the tax, the reason for collecting it, and how much I got for it. After that, I started watching for litterbugs. Most kids wanted to avoid detention, so to them, fifty cents was an even trade for my silence.

Recently, business has really dropped off. Hardly any kids leave trash behind now. Principal Jenkins thinks his policy is what turned the school around. The threat of detention was one reason. Paying my tax to avoid getting caught was a bigger one.

I do some stuff for free, too. (Cuz, you know, I'm not a monster.) I carry equipment to school rallies and assemblies, I move desks for teachers, and I help out the maintenance staff with stuff like moving bleachers or rolling out the big garbage bins on trash day. I like the maintenance people. They treat me like a normal kid just helping out.

But I guess I'm not a normal kid. I was born eleven pounds, twenty-six inches. Doesn't seem big until you consider that most babies are more like seven or eight pounds and nineteen or twenty inches when they're born. You get the idea. I was a big infant. Ninety-seventh-percentile big.

While most kids just stare, the only kid who never misses a chance to tell me I'm not normal is Stephen Hobert.

Stephen pronounces his name like he's French, but his family is from Springfield and I know for a fact he's never been to France. His mom is the head of the parents' association. She doesn't like students who stand out for "all the wrong reasons."

Stephen has a crew. I've seen them pick on kids.

Sixth graders are especially afraid of him (in a different way than they are afraid of me). They don't want to get on his bad side.

He draws pictures of people he doesn't like and sneaks them into their backpacks and lockers. I caught him once putting one of his masterpieces inside a girl's backpack. At lunch later that day the girl was crying with her friends as she showed them the drawing. I happened to see it as I walked to a lunch table. Stephen drew her like a stick figure with a big round head, bulging eyes, short hair, and a tie. Above the drawing, he wrote, "Is it a boy or a girl?"

Stephen uses words like someone throwing punches. Only it's nearly impossible to find the bruises. He's never been caught.

I don't collect garbage tax or cell phone storage fees from Stephen. I've thought long and hard about it. Sure, he had made a monster out of me by spreading rumors and just being his terrible self. But in a way, he's responsible for my biggest source of income—keeping kids away from him.

TWO

CROSSWALKS

When school is over, my four regulars plus the two new kids are waiting anxiously by the school entrance. They see me coming and light up with excitement. They know walking with me is saving them from a lot of torment.

"Let's go," I say. They all gather around and walk with me. They look like those ducklings from the picture book I used to read to my brother when he was little.

First, I drop off the curly-haired kid whose glasses are way too big for his face. They look like giant see-through dinner plates sitting on his nose. He's about a foot shorter than I am and as scrawny as a broomstick.

As we approach his house, the kid high-fives the others. He turns to me and waves.

"Thanks, Marcus," he says as his front gate opens and he walks inside. The gate closes and I continue to walk down the sidewalk.

The other kids are bouncing around me like remoras swimming under a great white. Occasionally they spot a fresh patch of snow, scoop some of it, and toss it at each other. They're careful not to hit me, and never walk too far behind.

When we reach the second kid's house, he runs inside without saying good-bye. He knocks on the front door, and his nanny opens it. She's got a baby in her arms. She pats the kid on the shoulder and ushers him inside. Then she waves at me and I nod.

Three more kids to drop off, then I'll walk back to the school library to finish my homework and wait for my brother.

"Hey, Marcus," one of the new kids says. "I used the map on my phone to find out exactly where Alex lives."

"Who?" I ask, not slowing my pace.

"Alex," he says, catching up and wagging his phone at me. "We procured your services earlier today?"

I stop.

The kid shows me his phone. He's mapped out walking directions to the other kid's house. It's about half a mile away, according to the map. I speed up and turn down a side street. The shuffling behind me tells me the kids are surprised by the sudden turn.

"Um, Marcus?"

I keep walking. "What?"

"Um, that's on the way to Cherry Hill Park," the kid says.

"So?" I tell him.

"So, that's where Stephen Hobert hangs out. His house is right next to it."

"So?"

"Um," he says, trying to keep up. "I just thought because, you know, we're trying to avoid—"

"We're not trying to avoid anything. It's a shortcut."

It'll take an extra twenty minutes if we follow the phone route. Add another ten to drop off the last kid. Then another ten minutes to walk back to the school library. That only gives me an hour to do my homework.

My brother is done with therapy at five. If I'm back later than five, he starts to get nervous. And his occupational therapist, Grace, has other patients to see.

I continue down the road toward Cherry Hill Park. It sounds like the kids are slowing their steps. I can tell by the way they're moving behind me that they're watching the park for Stephen and his crew. I walk past the snow-covered trees on the corner of the sidewalk. One of the kids rushes over to me and practically hugs my leg.

"Get off."

He does and we keep walking.

I can't blame them for wanting to stay clear of a punk like Stephen. He knows how to put a spotlight on the things kids worry most about themselves. At lunch, I hear him make comments about a kid's lisp, or say a boy will probably work in a gas station because he can't spell, or make fun of a kid's acne by calling her Crater Face. He makes fun of kids who have outdated clothes and phones. If a kid cries or threatens to tell on him, he says he's only joking and invites them to hang out. Most kids just try to stay away. But that doesn't always work. These aren't really things that teachers notice. Teachers don't know that he makes it a point to pick on the younger kids walking home. He doesn't take their money and usually doesn't shove them, but he ridicules them. Sometimes that hurts more. Sometimes that hurts longer.

I don't say anything the rest of the way. I drop the other two kids off and head down North Cherry Hill Drive to the final kid's house.

"I'm just up ahead there," he says, pointing to a two-story building close to Main Street.

"That's your house?" I ask him.

"Nah, that's where my mom works," he says. "She's a tax attor—"

"Thought you wanted me to take you home?"

"It'll save you some time if I just go there. You have to get back to school to pick up your brother, right?"

He points down the street. I nod.

"I've seen you guys walking home together," he says. "You live close by?"

I nod again. I'm kind of shocked he knows this.

"Maybe we can hang out? The three of us. Like a playdate or something."

"I don't do playdates."

"Right, well, thanks for walking me," he says.

"You can pay me half, then. For walking you halfway."

"Don't worry about it," he says.

"If I drop you off here, it's half. No free money."

He agrees. He starts to leave, but before he goes inside, I stop him.

"Hey."

He turns to face me.

"What's your name?" I ask him.

He looks around as if I was speaking to someone else.

"Um, Danny," he says. "It's Danny."

I nod and take off.

⊗⊗⊗

I finish my homework at 4:55. I leave my office in the library and walk out to the reception area. Ms. Mary, the librarian, waves at me and I nod at her. She smiles with her whole face. It's the kind of smile that makes you smile back even if you weren't in the mood before. She asks me if I was able to finish everything.

"Yes, thank you."

"I'm glad," she says. "Hey, Marcus?"

I stop and wait.

"How's your brother doing?"

"Good," I say.

"How's he adjusting to life in middle school?"

"Seems to like it," I say. "I think."

"Good. If you need anything, you know I'm here," she says. "I'll see you tomorrow."

"Good night," I tell her.

I walk to my locker and grab my things. My brother's therapist has an office next to the principal's. From behind me, a voice booms in my ear.

"Hi, Marcus!"

It's my brother, Charlie.

"Hey, buddy," I say, patting him on the shoulder. "I was just coming to get you. How was therapy?"

"Good. Smile! You promised."

I do my best.

"No. This is a smile. See?"

He grins and reveals a row of crooked teeth. He squeezes his eyes shut, causing his glasses to slide down the bridge of his nose. His brown top hat almost falls off his head. He snags it before it does, and places it carefully back on. This hat is basically part of my brother's school uniform. It's a replica Willy Wonka hat from *Willy Wonka and the Chocolate Factory*. The one starring Gene Wilder. He loves that movie.

"Try again," he says.

I curl my lips higher.

"Better," he says, and hugs me.

"Ready to go home?"

"Oh yeah."

I finish putting my books away and close my locker. Charlie pats me on the forearm and walks with me down the halls. He's about a foot shorter than I am. He smiles at the few students left in school as we pass them. He knows kids' names and makes it a point to call out to them.

"Hey, Tom! What's up, man?"

"Oh, hey, Charlie. Not much. Thanks."

He shakes Tom's hand and smiles brightly. Then he goes to another kid and waves.

"Hey, Christy! Cool shirt! Heart emoji. I have the sunglasses one! I am slick," he says, and mimics slicking back his hair.

He laughs and Christy responds with an awkward grin.

"Dude, don't say stuff like that," I tell him, moving him along.

"Why not? I do. I am slick. Ha!"

"You're ridiculous."

My brother keeps high-fiving students as we head outside. They return the high fives but don't really look at him, or me, for too long. Kids just prefer not to pay attention to us unless they have to.

It took a lot to get my brother into Montgomery Middle. There were parents who weren't thrilled about having a kid with Down syndrome in classes with other kids. Stephen's mom seemed to be the loudest opponent.

In the end, a large national association stepped in and put pressure on the school district to let him attend. There was already a special education class in the school, but Charlie became the first kid with Down syndrome to attend Montgomery Middle.

Principal Jenkins sent a letter home to every student's family saying it was the right of all children to receive a public education. My brother is in a few general education classes like PE and art and stuff, and he spends the rest of the school day in special education classes with kids who have different kinds of learning disabilities. He sees a speech therapist three times a week and an occupational therapist two times a week. I do most of my homework during his sessions.

"This way," Charlie says, leading us home.

My brother never forgets a place after he's been there once. He never gets lost.

"Man, we've walked this route a thousand times. I know that."

"Just checking." He looks at his watch. "You are going slow."

"No, I'm not," I tell him. "Hey, man, why don't you take off the Wonka hat and put your beanie on? It's getting cold."

"No. I want this hat. Because . . . ?"

"You love Willy Wonka."

"Yes!"

He starts singing as we walk.

"Don't sing it so fast," I tell him, tying a scarf around his neck. "I can't understand the lyrics when you do that."

He smiles and closes his eyes while he sings, stretching his arms wide and twirling around.

"Man, you're going to get run over by a car! Open your eyes."

He stops and looks at me. His glasses have slipped to the bridge of his nose again. He pokes my chest and leans so close that I can see his breath in the cold air.

"You are not fun."

I smack the top hat down and cover his eyes. "*You're* no fun," I tell him.

"No, you are no fun," he says, lifting the hat back onto his head.

"Man, fix your glasses. You look like a mad scientist."

He cracks up. Then he pushes his glasses back into place and makes a wacky face. I put my arm around his shoulders and he puts his arm around my waist.

We cross the large intersection, and the neighborhood starts to change. The houses get smaller. Closer together. We live on the corner in a little brown house that's about five blocks from the train station and forty-five minutes from the big city. It was my grandparents' house before they passed away. I take my brother's hand as we cross another street.

"Come on, buddy," I tell him. The last rays of sun disappear behind us as we walk on this chilly evening.

THREE
PURE IMAGINATION

I've lived in this house since I was two. I was born in Puerto Rico, where my dad's from, but I don't remember even the slightest thing about it. Charlie was born here in Springfield. He's never lived or been anywhere else.

The rest of the houses around here have a fence, but not our little brown house. Just a stone driveway that leads to a side entrance, where a rickety door always gives me trouble. I have to jam it a few times before it pops open. We walk in and take our shoes off in the mudroom. Charlie immediately runs upstairs.

"Hey, man, take your backpack with you."

"You bring it!" he yells from the top of the stairs.

I grab his backpack and walk up to his room. When I open his door, he's already in movie mode.

"Did you do your homework?"

Charlie ignores me and keeps messing with the remote control to get his movie to start playing.

"Yo, Mr. Wonka, did you hear me?"

He shoos me away.

"Seriously, Charlie," I tell him, bringing his backpack to his bed. "You're in middle school now. You gotta get your work done before you start watching stuff."

"I did it," he says, not looking at me.

"Really?"

"Yes! Go away."

I check his backpack and pull out his binder. I open his homework tab and check through the assignments. His handwriting has gotten way better, thanks to Grace. There are a few misspelled words, but it looks like he's doing pretty well. I check his math. He got all of it done. I see the last assignment is a book report. It's on Roald Dahl's *Charlie and the Great Glass Elevator*.

"You're reading it in class?"

"Yep," he says, still not looking.

"That's awesome, man." It's cool his teacher is trying to challenge him with the sequel to *Charlie and the Chocolate Factory*.

"How do you like it?"

"Good," he says.

"Cool. Wanna tell me about it?"

"No," he replies. "Go away. It is my relax time."

He shoos me off again, and this time I listen. On my way out, I pass the five-foot Stormtrooper cardboard cutout that he won shooting free throws at the town's Fourth of July festival last summer. Before I could tell him to let me shoot the ball, he clutched it in his left hand, kept his right smoothly on the side of the ball, and launched it in a perfect spin toward the hoop.

Nothing but net.

I remember the people behind me cheered and congratulated him. Charlie kept his left hand in the air with his wrist bent for emphasis. He had just made a basket and he wanted the guy at the booth to know it.

It was pretty awesome.

"Good shot, kid," he said, handing Charlie the Stormtrooper. "Wanna try your luck with another one?"

"Nah," Charlie said. "I swished one in your face."

My brother, the smack-talker.

I throw my backpack into my room and go downstairs to the kitchen. My mom left a note on the fridge. She works at the ticketing counter for a big airline at Philadelphia International Airport. Her commute is long, so I usually take care of the stuff at home.

Hey, hon,

They asked me to cover gate assignments, so (ugh) gonna be late.

**Hopefully not later than eight. (Fingers
crossed there aren't delays!)**

I left some food in the fridge.

**Please make sure Charlie bathes. And tell
him to wear his bathrobe! It's supposed
to drop down to the twenties tonight. And
text me if there's an emergency. Or if you
just want to talk. ☺**

> **I love you both.
> Go team go ☺**

My mom ends every note with *Go team go*. She calls
my brother and me her all-star team.

She's been working at the airline for over ten years.
She started off as a reservations associate, then moved
to gate agent after Charlie was born. Mom wants to get
her business degree so she can get promoted, earn
more money, and have a better schedule. I think she
feels guilty that she works morning shifts and sometimes has to work at night and doesn't get to see us. She
leaves long notes about how much she loves us and how
she's going to get a promotion and take us on vacation
and all that. She's always stressing.

I take out my earnings for the day and put them on

the kitchen counter. I count out fourteen dollars. Not bad for a day's work. I walk over to the Cookie Monster jar and drop in the cash. My mom calls it our Cookie Monster Cash. She adds whatever change and loose singles she has, but she doesn't know I do too. She thinks the money she's dropping in is just adding up.

Last spring my brother and I came home from hanging out at the playground and found the entire bottom floor of the house flooded. A leaky pipe had dripped water all day and messed up the carpets. When the repair guy came, he said it was going to cost over three hundred dollars to fix the pipe. My mom asked the guy if he could fix the leak now and she would pay him at the end of the week when she got her paycheck. The guy said he'd only agree if he could take her out on a date.

We had a leaky pipe for a week. Charlie loved it. He splashed around, acting like he was a pirate on a sinking ship. We decided to create the Cookie Monster Cash relief jar so we could have cash in case of emergencies. Soon after, I started my businesses at school, and I've been secretly adding cash to the jar ever since. Our heating unit busted right at the start of winter, and luckily we had enough to pay for it without my mom having to deal with another creepy guy.

I close the cash jar and open the refrigerator. I don't know why my mom insists on leaving peanut butter in there. She says it can go bad, but all it does is get hard and impossible to spread. I scoop out a lump of peanut butter and dump it into a bowl. I grab some honey from the cupboard and squeeze it in. I pop it into the microwave and set it for thirty seconds. The beeping echoes through the house, and I hear Charlie crawling under the table and moving between the chairs.

"I know you're under the table," I tell him, watching the microwave warm up my peanut butter. "You think you're slick, trying to sneak up on me?"

He's giggling, but I don't turn around. The microwave beeps a few times when it's done, and I take out the bowl, throw a few Ritz Crackers in, and grab a spoon. I walk toward the dinner table, knowing Charlie is under there and ready to pounce. By now he's laughing so hard, he can barely contain himself. He would be the worst undercover agent ever.

I look under the table, but he's not there. I hear footsteps in the kitchen. I hear him trying to sneak up behind me. With every step, he gets closer and giggles louder. Right when he's inches from pouncing, he holds his breath and I can see from the reflection of the plates hanging in the dining room that he's crouching down and about to leap. He gets ready to spring.

"AHHHH!!!!"

He jumps behind me and my chair tilts forward.

"Yo! You're gonna knock me down, man!" I say, putting the bowl of peanut butter on the table.

When I stand, he dives for my legs and clings to my knees. I buckle and fall to the floor. Charlie climbs up to my shoulders and digs his hands into my sides, trying to tickle me.

"I got you, Marcus!"

He knows my tickle spot and digs his fingers in relentlessly.

"Hey, man, that really tickles!" I squirm around, laughing as he continues to move his fingers right under my shoulder. I roll over and flatten him on the ground.

"Ahhh!!! You're . . . uuu . . ." He lies flat on the ground, completely still.

I quickly get up, thinking he can't breathe. His eyes are closed.

"Hey, man. You okay? You okay, buddy?"

He doesn't move. I start feeling nervous. I check his face and it's still. I'm about a hundred pounds heavier than he is. He's probably out of breath. I put my head down to his chest to check his breathing. He had heart surgery when he was an infant. The doctor says he's fine now, but it still worries me sometimes. I check his heartbeat. When I do, he sneak attacks me, jamming his fingers under my armpit and wiggling them.

"GOTCHA!!!"

He moves with expert speed, and I can't help tumbling to the floor, cracking up. He jumps on top of me and continues to tickle.

"Mercy, mercy!" I say, trying to stop laughing.

"Who is your master?"

"You are!" I tell him as he continues to tickle. "You are!"

"WHO. IS. YOUR. MASTER?!"

I can't stop laughing. The more I do, the more powerless I am. He totally got me.

"You. Please, Charlie. Please! Mercy! Mercy!"

He finally stops and stands up, his two hands in fists resting at his sides. He smiles triumphantly and reaches a hand out to help me. I take it and roll up to standing, using him for balance.

"You got me good, Charlie. You got me real good."

"Yep," he says, going to the table to scoop some peanut butter from my bowl.

"Did you do your homework?" he asks.

"Yeah," I tell him.

"Watch *Wonka* with me."

"Thought you wanted to watch it alone."

"Come with me and you see . . . in pure imagination!" he says, trying to sing the song.

"Why don't we change it up a little? Let's watch *Hulk*."

"I watch *Hulk* every day."

"What?"

"You're the Hulk and I tickle him!"

Charlie goes for my armpits again, but he can't reach when I'm standing. I pretend to laugh, but he knows it doesn't tickle me for real.

"I will get you when you are sleeping," he says, and puts two fingers to his eyes then points at me. Then he laughs and hugs me. I put my arm around him and hug him back.

"All right, we can watch *Wonka* again, but you have to take a bath. Mom says."

Charlie slumps over and grunts his disapproval. "I get water in my ears."

"I know, man, but do like I told you, cup your hands over your ears when you get water in them and then pump the water out."

Charlie copies the motion I make with my hands and pumps his ears.

"Go, and then we'll watch the movie and eat dinner." He doesn't move.

"Come on, man. Don't you want to watch *Wonka*?"

He still doesn't move. This is one of the things Charlie does when he doesn't want to do something. He just stays still. But it's only because he's thinking about it. He wants to be convinced that what I'm asking of him is worth it. I respect that.

"Okay, I'll make sure you don't get water in your ears when you take a bath."

He thinks about it for a minute. When he sees me walking over to the bathroom, he starts to follow. He waits outside in the hall and watches as I crouch down to turn on the water and fill the tub. I move my mom's stuff to the bathroom sink and make room for Charlie to sit. I squeeze some body wash into the tub and move my hand around the bottom until bubbles start forming.

Bubbles are all it takes to convince Charlie. He runs inside and starts to take off his socks.

"Okay, okay. You can leave. I don't need you."

I stand up and step back to the door.

"Off you go," he says, waving me away.

I leave Charlie in the bathroom and head to my room.

❊❊❊

Later that evening I heat up two big bowls of chicken soup in the microwave and Charlie reads a sports magazine at the dinner table.

"I want to do this," he says, pointing to the picture of a guy running.

"You want to run track?"

"Yes. And this."

He points to a picture of a football player.

"Football? No way, man," I say. "Hey, what about this?" I show him an article about sports writing.

"*Meh*," he says. "I am a man of action." He points to the magazine, at a picture of a track star wearing a gold medal. "I am the greatest!"

I laugh. "Come on, man. Let's go watch *Wonka*."

We go to Charlie's room and he clicks on the remote to start the movie. I grab the two bowls of soup and we watch quietly in his room.

❂❂❂

When Charlie is asleep a few hours later, I hear someone at the door. I sit up from the chair in Charlie's room and hear my mom push her way inside the house. I walk down the stairs and find her taking off her coat quickly in the mudroom to get inside where it's warm.

"Man, it is cold outside!" she says, shivering.

I go to the kitchen to heat her food.

"Hey, sweetheart. What are you still doing up?"

"Waiting for you," I say, staring at the microwave spinning my mom's bowl of soup. "How was work?"

"They had to de-ice three planes. Ugh, that delayed everything. I'm sorry I'm so late."

I take out the bowl and walk it over to the table, where Mom's placing her bag down and getting ready to sit.

"Oh, sweetie," she says, taking the bowl of soup. "Thank you."

I nod and sit next to her.

"Did your brother bathe?"

I nod. "I got him with soap bubbles."

"Nice!" She swirls her soup before taking a sip. "Yum, nothing like warm soup on a cold night."

I don't say anything. I just quietly watch her eat. The sound of the spoon hitting the edge of the bowl sounds like a bell. She sets the spoon on the table and raises the bowl to her lips. She slurps the last of the noodles, carrots, and broth until it's all gone. She puts the bowl back down and wipes the side of her face with the back of her hand. There's a loose noodle stuck to the side of the bowl and she carefully pinches it, dangling it above her face before letting it drop into her mouth.

"I was hungry," she says. She takes a final look inside the bowl but doesn't find any loose carrots or noodles. She takes a sip of water and watches me watching her. She smiles and puts her hand on mine.

"How was school?"

"Good," I tell her.

"Good," she says.

"I should get to bed," I say.

"Okay, sweetheart," she says, rubbing my hand.

"Good night, Mom. Love you."

"Love you too, sweetheart. *Go—*"

"*Team go,*" I say, and walk to my room. I hear my mom rummaging through the kitchen, saying something about peanut butter going bad. Then I hear a drawer open and the sound of silverware rattling. A utensil clanks against glass, and after a moment the microwave beeps. She opens the refrigerator, and I know she's put the peanut butter back in there. After a moment I hear her walking up the stairs. She opens the door to my room and pops her head inside. I look up and she smiles, a spoonful of peanut butter in her mouth. She mumbles, "I love you," then heads to Charlie's room. I know she'll cuddle up with him. She always falls asleep halfway on the bed with her uniform on. Sometimes I get up in the middle of the night, put a comforter over her, and move her leg onto his bed.

Go team go.

FOUR
TRIGGER

I wake up the next morning and get ready to walk my clients. My mom usually drops off Charlie at school because he doesn't have class until ten. It's cold outside, but I don't mind. I get hot easily. My mom says I'm a heat giver. The cold just doesn't bother me, that's all.

I walk about ten blocks toward the gas station and past the mechanic shop. They don't open until eight o'clock. A few more blocks and I reach Main Street. The shops are closed except for a few coffee places that people walk in and out of sleepily. The sun is barely starting to shine in the sky, and there's an orange-pink glow down Main Street. I turn onto Danny's street and walk a few more blocks. When I get to his house, he's already waiting outside his door, his backpack on. He looks like he's about to turn into an icicle.

"Good morning," he says, shivering.

"Why are you sitting out here?"

"So you wouldn't have to wait," he says, standing up.

BIENVENIDOS A NUESTRA CASA is embroidered on the doormat.

"What does that mean?" I ask.

"You don't speak Spanish?"

"No, why would I?"

"I just thought because you were half Puerto Rican . . . Never mind. It means 'Welcome to our house.'"

"You're Spanish?" I ask.

"My grandparents are from Colombia," he says.

Danny must drink coffee in the morning, because he doesn't stop talking about his family the entire way to school. "Hurry up," I say, ignoring him.

"You, um, you ever get to Puerto Rico?" he asks, once he catches up to me.

"Not since I was born," I say. "And that's the end of that conversation."

"Okay," he says.

We walk in silence back toward Main Street and cross to the side of town with the biggest houses in the neighborhood.

"Hey, Marcus?" Danny asks me.

"What?"

"Thanks for agreeing to walk me."

"You're paying me to do it."

"I know, but still," he says. "Thank you. It's tough sometimes when you're the only kid in your grade who watches *Jeopardy!* and plays card games with your grandparents."

"Huh?"

"I like them, though, you know?"

"What?"

"My grandparents."

"My grandparents are dead," I tell him.

"Oh," he says, suddenly stopping. "Both sides?"

"Yep. I have a great-uncle on my dad's side in Puerto Rico, but I haven't spoken to my da— You need to stop asking questions."

Danny stays quiet for a moment. "I talk too much."

"Yes, you do."

We scoop up the rest of the kids and get to school before the first bell rings. The kids run off to their classrooms, and I start making my way to my locker.

I get to my locker and carefully place my business binder inside. I take out my history book and notebooks and organize them in my backpack. When I shut the locker door, I notice Stephen Hobert silently watching me.

"You know," he says, talking to one of his friends, "I wonder why Charlie Vega gets to come to school late when the rest of us have to be here so early? Isn't that kind of messed up?"

I glare at Stephen.

"I mean, *everybody* fought to get him into school. Well, not everybody. And he gets to choose his own schedule?"

Soon a small crowd gathers around us. Stephen is smirking.

"So, Gigantor," Stephen says. "Where's your brother?" He mimics the hand gestures my brother makes sometimes. I can feel blood rushing to my fists.

I try to keep cool about most things. When you're as big as me, you can't get rattled easily or you'll scare people. But make fun of my brother, and all bets are off. That's not me being a bully. That's me being real.

"What is that you're saying?"

"I didn't say anything," I tell him, trying to make my voice sound big and frightening. But it's not. It's not coming out like I want it to.

"Are you threatening me? Because it looks like you're trying to threaten me."

My fingernails dig into my palms, but I can't speak.

Stephen continues. "See this, guys? The bully is threatening me. He takes money from little kids and now he's threatening me also."

His friends gather around and watch me.

"Your brother should've never come to this school.

Half a year of taxpayer dollars for some re—"

"Don't," I say, clenching my jaw and stepping closer to him. "Don't you dare say that word."

He backs up and his friends follow.

"What word, Vega?" Stephen asks.

"Don't, Marcus." Danny suddenly breaks through the crowd and stands next to me. "He's baiting you," he whispers. "Don't pay attention."

"You're such a waste of space, Gigantor," Stephen taunts. "I mean, all that size and you can't even dribble a basketball. Your mom and dad must be . . . Oh wait, that's right. Your dad went to another country and never came back."

"Puerto Rico is part of the United States, you igno-ramus!" Danny blurts.

"What did you call me?" Stephen angles himself to-ward Danny.

I put my hand on Danny's shoulder and move him behind me. "It's not worth it," I say as I start to turn around.

Stephen leans in and whispers just outside of ear-shot of everyone else.

"No wonder he likes you," he says. "Your brother and him are just alike. Both a couple of . . ."

Barely anybody hears it. But I do. Stephen Hobert says the one word that sends me into a blind rage. It's the one word that causes an avalanche on the mountain inside of me. I turn around, my fists clenched, and I send Stephen crashing into the lockers across the hall. The sound makes everyone watching jump. He slumps to the ground while students back away. A teacher runs in and looks from me to Stephen. A few kids point in my direction. Others shake their heads. Most stay quiet. I don't see Danny. I don't see anyone. I look back at Stephen. His mouth is bloody. His cheeks are red. He holds his chin while the teacher examines him. Then he points. The teacher turns to me. Stephen smirks through bloody teeth.

FIVE

TROUBLE WITH A CAPITAL T

My mom is called into the principal's office just as she's dropping off Charlie on her way to work. Before she steps in, she calls her boss. She ends up having to use a sick day. Stephen's parents rush to the school soon after and storm into the office. Stephen's dad paces around angrily while I sit in a chair and stare out the window behind Principal Jenkins. Stephen's mom hasn't stopped applying an ice pack to her son's jaw.

"You okay, baby?" she says over and over again. "You okay?"

Stephen's dad walks over to the window. I know he's staring at me to try to get my attention. Our principal is on the phone, talking to someone, but it's hard to know who it is. He looks over to me. My knuckle hurts a little. I can feel it pulsating. I didn't know punching someone could hurt so much. I've never punched anyone before.

"Okay," our principal finally says. "Thank you."

He hangs up and a door opens. My mom walks in. She looks at me and her face sinks. She squints like she does when she's really worried about something. I know this expression well.

"Please have a seat, Ms. Vega."

"Thank you," she says, and takes the chair next to me. Stephen's dad continues to pace.

"Please have a seat, Mr. Hobert."

"I'm fine standing, David. Thank you."

Principal Jenkins seems a little irked at being called by his first name, but he doesn't say anything. He continues.

"Okay, let's talk about the incident between these two—"

"I'll talk about it," Stephen's mom says, interrupting. "That brute of a boy assaulted my son! He broke his jaw. We are demanding the severest possible punishment from the school. Once we take Stephen to the hospital, we'll see how much the medical damages will be." She glares at my mom. "Clearly that boy doesn't have any positive male role models in his life. Just look at my son! Just look at him!"

My mom doesn't say anything. I see her picking at her cuticles. She looks at Principal Jenkins, who offers her a quiet nod.

"Well, what do you have to say for yourself, young man?" Stephen's father says, pointing at me.

I don't say anything. I stare at Principal Jenkins.

"Answer me!"

Principal Jenkins jumps in.

"Hold on there, Mr. Hobert. These are my students. I'll be leading this discussion."

"You'd better," Stephen's dad says.

"Have a seat, Jim," our principal says as he stands up and moves around his desk. He's tall and wide and he has a crew cut. Like me, only he has gray hair. He sits on the edge of his desk and folds his arms.

"Okay, let's talk about this," he says. Stephen begins by telling his side of the story.

He says I've been taking money from little kids and hiding their phones from them and collecting money for storage. He says I make kids give me money when I catch them throwing garbage on the floor and that I shove kids into lockers. He says I walk around intimidating everyone at school.

Then he says that he saw me picking on a sixth grader today and decided to intervene. According to him, I pushed him then punched him in the face when he told me to leave the kid alone. Principal Jenkins asks about the kid. Stephen says he can't remember his name.

"It was all a blur, sir."

Stephen's mom kept stroking her son's hair the entire time, while his dad shook his head in disbelief. My mom didn't interrupt at all. Finally, Principal Jenkins turns to me.

"All right, Marcus. Let's hear your side."

I don't say anything. I just look out the window behind our principal's desk.

"Marcus?"

I look at Principal Jenkins. He stays focused on me even as I look away. My mom still doesn't say anything.

"Marcus, we have a zero-tolerance policy for bullying at this school. Stephen is saying a whole lot of stuff here that troubles me. And the fact that he's injured isn't helping your cause. If you don't answer, I'm going to assume this is how the events transpired. Is what Stephen has said true?"

I shake my head.

"No?" he asks.

"No," I say.

"He's lying! Look at my son!"

"Mrs. Hobert, please. Your son spoke. Now it's Marcus's turn."

Stephen's mom lets out a huff and sits back in her seat.

I make eye contact with Principal Jenkins again.

"Go ahead, Marcus."

"He . . . I don't know, man. He picks on kids."

"Liar!" Mrs. Hobert says. "You're the one! Look at how big you are—"

"That doesn't make him a bully," my mom suddenly interrupts Mrs. Hobert. Everyone looks at her. "It doesn't," she says. "He takes care of his brother every day after school. He gets good grades. He's never been called into the office."

"Well, ask your *perfect* son if he's taking money from kids," Stephen's mom scoffs.

My mom looks at me. "Are you taking money from kids?"

I nod.

"See!" Mrs. Hobert says.

"But," I say, "I'm not *taking* it. They're paying me."

Our principal stands up from his desk and crosses his arms.

"Paying you? For what?"

I list all of my businesses. When Stephen's mom says I'm lying again, I hand Principal Jenkins my spiral with the tabs of all my businesses and the dates I collected money plus the person I collected money from. He takes a while to look through it. Stephen's dad gets up and tries to peek, but our principal closes my binder and puts it on his desk.

"Why are you collecting this money?"

"Cookie Monster Cash," I reply.

"Marcus," my mom says, and I see her eyes getting all puffy. "No, baby. No."

"Wait, this kid created businesses related to school regulations? That's pretty clever," Stephen's dad says, nodding.

"Jim! He hurt our boy!" Mrs. Hobert clearly isn't done yelling. "He broke his jaw!"

"His jaw's not broken, Maureen," Stephen's dad replies.

"All right, everybody, calm down," Principal Jenkins interrupts. My mom hasn't changed the worried, quiet look on her face since she walked in. "Marcus, why did you hit Stephen?"

"Because he's a bully!" Stephen's mom interjects again. The principal shoots her a look, but she keeps jawing for justice. "Something better be done," she says, "or the school board is going to hear about it."

"Thank you for the reminder, Mrs. Hobert," the principal says. "Marcus?"

"He said the *R* word," I whisper.

"What's that?" Principal Jenkins leans in close.

"The *R* word. He called my brother and this other kid the *R* word. So I punched him."

Principal Jenkins looks at Stephen. "Is that true?"

"No!"

Our principal keeps asking questions and finally finds out who the other kid is in this situation. He has no choice but to call in Danny to get the story straight.

"I was right next to the plaintiff when this incident occurred," Danny says, standing next to me.

"The plaintiff, meaning Mr. Hobert?" says Principal Jenkins.

"I was standing right next to the defendant," Danny corrects, "when the incident occurred. The plaintiff did indeed use a derogatory word to speak about the defendant's brother and myself."

"This isn't a trial, Mr. Peña," our principal says. "You don't need to speak like that."

"My apologies, Your Honor, I mean, sir."

"Thank you," Principal Jenkins says. "You can go back to class."

Danny leaves and our principal stands up again.

"Okay," he says. "This is what's going to happen. Marcus, you are suspended until further notice. We will look at the details of this incident and consider all punishments, including expulsion."

Stephen's mom gives a weird standing ovation. "Finally, some justice."

"And, Mr. Hobert," the principal says to Stephen, "it sounds like you've been harassing younger students at this school. You will serve detention and community service for one week. We do not tolerate hateful language."

"You've got to be kidding me. This is not the end of this," Mrs. Hobert warns. "Not by a long shot."

She storms out of the office with Stephen and his dad.

We get up to leave, but Principal Jenkins stops us.

"Hang on a sec," he says.

He closes the door and says he wants to talk to us about Charlie.

"I worry," he says, "that Marcus's need to protect his brother may cause him to jeopardize his own schooling."

"What do you mean, Mr. Jenkins?" my mom asks.

"Look, I know your son isn't a bully, Ms. Vega. This kid helps out around the school, sets up for assemblies. He never complains. I do want you to stop making money off my rules, though. Do you understand?"

He points to my binder.

"That's gotta be the first time in my thirty-plus years . . . Unbelievable," he says, shaking his head. "Anyway, no more moneymaking schemes. Okay?"

I nod.

"I know Marcus is a good kid, Ms. Vega," he says to my mom. "I know it can't be easy raising two boys."

"I don't see how that's relevant," my mom says, raising an eyebrow.

"Point taken." Mr. Jenkins rubs the back of his head.

"Look, spring break is next week. I suggest taking some time to regroup and rethink some of Charlie's educational goals."

"What do you mean?"

The principal goes to his desk and pulls out a brochure. He hands it to my mom. She looks at it, and when she turns it over, I read the front: *The Academy for Exceptional Students*.

"It is a highly regarded school for individuals with special needs. They have academies all over the country."

"There isn't one anywhere near here," my mom says, flipping through the brochure.

"There's one in DC. That's about two and a half hours away."

"What are you saying?" my mom asks.

"Are you kicking my brother out of school?" I finally blurt out. "Because of me?"

"No!" he says, then turns to my mom. "Look, I just thought you should see that there are options out there for Charlie that would allow both children to thrive individually."

"Thank you, Mr. Jenkins," my mom says, handing the brochure back. "But my sons are fine here. We're fine."

My mom collects her bag and takes my hand.

"Ms. Vega," Principal Jenkins says, insisting she

take the brochure. "Just look at it. Please. It could be a good fit for your family."

"You know, Mr. Jenkins, you fought really hard to make a place for Charlie at this school."

"I did," he says, "and now I'm looking out for Marcus."

"I can take care of myself," I say.

"You're not a grown man, Marcus. You're a kid. And I don't want you to get into more trouble, trying to be your brother's savior."

I don't like what Principal Jenkins is saying, but I can tell from his eyes that he believes he's doing the right thing.

"You know what? I'm taking my other son home as well," my mom says. "I hope you're happy."

Principal Jenkins shakes his head and tries to say something, but my mom has already walked off. I follow her outside to get Charlie.

"What are you doing here?" Charlie asks as my mom collects his things at his classroom. "What are you doing?"

"We're going home, sweetie," she replies.

"It's schooltime," he says. "I'm in school now."

"I know, buddy, but we're going to go home to spend some time together."

We leave and Charlie continues to ask where we're going. He doesn't like when things change suddenly. We hop in my mom's car, and the school disappears into the distance. My brother looks around, still wondering why he's going home. My mom focuses on the road and doesn't say anything.

I look at my hands. My right hand is swollen and the cold has started to crack the skin.

SIX
THE *IF* FACTOR

My mom was real young when she had me. She was in college when she met my dad, they got married, and then I was born. I don't remember much about my dad, but sometimes I see flashes in my head that feel so familiar. Like my dad making funny faces at me as I sit at a table, eating peas or something. I see him making these faces while sticking out his ears and bouncing around. I guess he's trying to make me laugh because I won't eat the peas. I see him take my spoon and pretend to eat my food. Saying, "Mío. Esto es mío." I don't know Spanish, but I somehow know he's saying my food is his. Then he gives me the spoon, and younger me scarfs down the peas.

I don't remember my parents fighting or why they

even split up in the first place. My mom never talks about it. As I got older I figured that he just didn't feel like being around. Maybe he was ashamed or something. That thought made me angry. It pulled at me *and* kept me stuck in one place at the same time.

I look up and catch my mom watching me carefully from the doorway. I wonder how long she's been standing there.

"Hey," she says.

"Hey," I reply.

"So, I should be pretty mad at you."

"Yeah."

"I have to take a week off of work, possibly more."

I nod.

"Your principal is suggesting a private school for your brother because of how you behaved today."

I don't respond.

"And this new school happens to cost about a quarter of my yearly salary."

I stare at the chipped crown molding wrapped around my bedroom. The powder-blue walls that my mom swears one day we're going to repaint. The window that never shuts completely. The gray sky outside. The way the light casts a shadow across the wood floor. It reaches all the way to my desk from the entrance of my room.

"We really need to repaint this room," my mom says for the hundredth time. And for the hundredth time, I tell her I don't care.

"Don't you want any posters at least?"

I tell her no. My room doesn't have a lot of stuff in it. Honestly, clutter bothers me. I have a desk. A chair. A computer. That's about it. I have a few framed pictures of Charlie and me and some of my mom. In my closet, I have a bag of old stuffed animals. I keep meaning to give them away now that Charlie is too old for them, but I haven't gotten around to it.

"This isn't working, is it?" my mom says.

I finally look at Mom to try to understand what she means.

"I work too much. We're always trying to fix something around this old house, and saving money in case something else breaks—which, by the way, no more side businesses, okay?"

"Okay."

"I mean, Mr. Jenkins is right, you know? You're a kid. I'm putting all this responsibility on you and you're fourteen years old. What kind of mom am I?"

"Don't worry about that, Mom," I tell her. "Forget what he said. He doesn't know us."

"No, sweetie," she says. "You shouldn't have to do all that. Look what happened. You're crumbling under the weight of it all."

"I'm fine, Mom."

"No, you're not," she says. "We need to get away from here and out of this rut. Just the three of us. We need to regroup."

"Where are we going to go? We don't have money for a trip."

"One of the great things about my job is that we can fly for free if we really want to. Where would you like to go?"

"Puerto Rico," I say. My mouth fires off before my thoughts can catch up.

"Now, why would you want to go there?"

"You know why," I tell her.

"To visit your dad? No! Goodness no."

"Why not?" I reply. "You just said that you work too much and everything's always broken and everything's a mess." I could feel my face getting hot. "Why shouldn't he help us?"

"Because your father has had plenty of opportunities to help and he hasn't, Marcus. Not once."

"But have you called him? Sent him pictures? Told him to come visit?"

"Marcus, we're not going to see your father. Okay? End of discussion."

I look out the window and ignore her.

"But," she says, walking over to me and placing her hands on my shoulders, "Puerto Rico isn't a bad idea.

We could fly for free and stay with your great-uncle Ermenio in Old San Juan."

"The guy who sends the Christmas cards every year with five bucks for me and Charlie?"

"Yeah," she says. "I loved spending time with him when your dad and I were together. He hasn't seen you since you were a baby. And he's only seen pictures of Charlie. I could call him," my mom says. She sounds serious.

"So, we could stay with Great-uncle Ermenio and go see Dad."

My mom takes a seat at the edge of my bed and pulls at my toes. She's done this since I was little.

"Honey, your dad moves around a lot. And I only have an email for him. The chances of him responding are zero to none."

"But if we're going to go . . ."

"We haven't even made the decision to go! We're just talking."

"Mom, we have to go," I say, sitting up. "What if that school for Charlie is really good? What if Dad can help us pay for it?"

"Marcus, what are you going on about? The closest school is in DC. Are we supposed to move?"

I shrug. "Why not? What do we have here anyway?"

My mom scoots close to me. "This house, honey. We can't just move."

"What if you got a job in DC? What about . . . I don't know."

I notice my mom has been holding the brochure Principal Jenkins gave her. Maybe she's been thinking about it like I have.

"Can I see that?" I ask, reaching out. My mom hands it to me.

"Look, there's one in New York, two in Boston, one in St. Louis," I say, pointing. "There's even one in Miami. We can move anywhere, Mom. You work at one of the biggest airlines in the world. You can get transferred. And Dad can help us pay for Charlie's school. We can get out of this town."

"Honey, honey, relax. Look, a lot happened today." My mom exhales.

"Can you call work?" I ask. "See if you can get us a flight? Call Uncle Ermenio. . . ."

"Marcus . . ."

"Then email Dad. . . ."

"Whoa, slow down. First, you're suspended. You should be grounded, not thinking about vacation."

"Come on—"

"Second," my mom interrupts, "suddenly you have this interest in seeing your father?"

I nod.

"Why?"

"I dunno," I say, looking at my closet door.

My mom grows quiet for what feels like a really long time. Then she lets out a big exaggerated breath.

"Let me think about it," she finally says. "But don't get your hopes up."

"I won't."

"*If* we end up going. *If*. It's not definite. *If*." My mom points to me. "I want this to be a reset for us. You. Your brother. And me. Got it?"

"Got it," I say, feeling excited.

"If," she repeats. "*If* we go."

"Right," I say. "If."

My mom walks out of my room and I hear her talking to herself again.

"A chance for us to get out of our routine," she mutters. "Spend time together as a team."

"Hey, Mom?" I say, getting up and going to my computer.

"Yeah?" She turns to face me.

"Where was the last place he was at?"

"Marcus, are you even listening to me?"

"Yes, family vacation. Go team go. So, do you remember?"

"The last place was at your uncle Ermenio's house in Old San Juan."

"Do you have an address?" I ask, typing "Old San Juan, Puerto Rico" into Google.

"Bordering on annoying now, Marcus. You're bordering."

"Come on, Mom," I tell her. "Aren't you even a little curious to see where he is?"

"I'm not even sure I can get three plane tickets, Marcus. And what if Ermenio doesn't have room for us? There are a lot of *ifs* to figure out."

"Okay," I say, still browsing online.

My mom pecks me on the cheek and leaves my room. I search my computer for a while longer and finally turn it off and head to bed. I don't know why my dad never answers my mom's emails.

I hadn't thought about connecting with my father. But now I want to send him an email. He might respond if he knew we were coming. It's another *if* that needs an answer.

SEVEN
PRESSING SEND

The next morning, I step into my closet, pull out my sneakers, and lace them up. I got a new pair of kicks for Christmas, and they're already starting to wear down. Some kids have six or seven pairs of sneakers. They like to show them off. I see them bragging to each other during lunchtime. Especially Stephen. He comes in with a new pair every other week. I have a few, but I usually wear the newer ones consistently for about a month straight. Every day. I like the way they mold to my feet the more I use them. It's like the shoes get comfortable with me and vice versa. We fit better the more time we spend together. Anyway, what's the point of having shoes that are barely used? I bet Stephen doesn't use his sneakers more than four or five times, if that.

My mom walks by and stops at my door, nearly spilling her coffee.

"Whoa! Just where do you think you're going, mister?"

"Walking the kids to school," I tell her as I finish getting ready.

"Marcus, did you hear anything that Principal Jenkins said yesterday? No more business ventures."

"Mom, these kids paid through the end of the week. That's today," I tell her. "I have to fulfill my obligation to them."

"Marcus, you are *charging* kids to walk them to school. Do you not see the problem with that?"

"They asked me to do it," I reply. "And I give them a fair price."

"You are not a private security company! Marcus, honey, this isn't a joke."

"I never said it was," I say. I can tell my mom is getting frustrated. She starts to rub her neck, which has gotten red. Mine gets like that when I'm angry too. "I have to honor my commitment," I tell her. "It's just today. Then that's it."

My mom watches me carefully, then shakes her head. "Marcus, we have to lay low. I'm worried. I really want you to stay out of sight while all of this gets sorted out."

"Just today, Mom. I promise."

She exhales, then takes a sip of her coffee. "Okay. Just be careful. Stephen's mom is looking for any opportunity—"

"I will," I say as I pass her to get to the stairs.

"Grace said she would do a house visit later for Charlie."

"Cool," I say.

"She's really great," Mom says, walking down the stairs. She watches me as I start outside. I turn around before I leave.

"I'm sorry for all that went down, Mom," I say.

"You shouldn't have punched him, Marcus. That's never a good solution. I'm worried now that the kids you're walking—"

"Those kids wouldn't say anything," I tell her. "When they walk with me, Stephen doesn't pick on them."

"That's what I'm afraid of," she says. "That he's going to be waiting around to taunt you."

"Don't worry, Mom. It'll be fine."

I see the concern on her face. She thinks Stephen is going to push me over the limit again.

"Expulsions stay on your permanent record, Marcus." I can tell that she's trying to stall.

"Mom, I gotta go. I'm going to be late."

"And you're so smart. You'll be able to get into any good school."

I'm going to high school next year. It's why I've been

thinking that maybe the academy would be better for Charlie. When I graduate, he's going to be left alone in middle school. Stephen won't be there anymore, but there's always another Stephen waiting in the wings.

"You know what? I'm going to start looking into our family trip," she declares. "I think there might be a silver lining to all of this."

"Cool," I tell her, and give her a kiss on the cheek before finally heading out.

"Be careful, sweetie," she says.

"I will," I tell her.

My mom looks at me over the rim of her coffee cup as she takes a sip. Then I hear her close the door behind me.

The cold air hardens my cheeks as I make my way to Danny's house. When I get there, he's on his lawn, throwing little twigs at a tree.

"What are you doing?" I ask.

"Oh, hey!" he says, dropping the twigs and walking over. "I was, um, I was playing Dragonlord. These are my fire sticks." He points to the branches on the brown patch of grass in his yard.

"Ready?" I say.

"Um, are you sure that's a good idea?" he says, putting the stick down. "Principal Jenkins said you couldn't—"

"Let's go," I tell him, starting to walk.

"Really, I can walk myself. It's not a big deal."

"You paid me," I tell him. "No freebies."

I'm already late to pick up the other kids, so I hurry. Danny's feet move faster to keep up. I map out a route in my head that will save me a few minutes. I make a plan to drop the kids off at the corner of the school and wait until they get in safely.

"Hey," Danny says, almost jogging to keep up. "I started a petition after you left yesterday to get you back into school. All the sixth graders signed it."

I ask him why he's helping me.

"I don't have any siblings," he says. "Or too many friends. Plus, I believe in justice."

We keep walking to the other kids' houses, and one by one they come running out to greet me. They're excited I'm walking them, but they're also worried I'm going to get into trouble. I tell them the same thing I told Danny: a job is a job. They bounce around excitedly, asking what it felt like to punch someone and how many times I have knocked someone out. They're surprised when I tell them it was the first time I ever did that. Then they're surprised I'm actually talking to them.

"You've never said more than three words to me," one kid marvels.

"I feel so important all of a sudden," another one says.

"Gentlemen," Danny interrupts. "Give him some space."

Danny tells them that they have to keep petitioning the school to claim justice. He tells them that Stephen cannot continue to get away with this psychological torment.

Danny talks like he's forty years old.

We're about a block away from school when the kids stop. It's Stephen. His mom gets out of the car with him and holds up the drop-off line. She puts her hand up at the other cars like she's annoyed at all the honking. She walks him into school and gives him a kiss on the cheek and rubs his back. After Stephen goes inside, I tell the kids with me to go.

"Meet me here at three," I tell them. They all agree. Danny stays behind.

"Thanks, Marcus," he says.

I nod.

❂❂❂

It's the weekend and the official start of spring break. Break is early this year, so it's still cold outside. Mom hadn't mentioned our trip in a couple of days, and it was looking more and more like we weren't going to go. Suddenly she calls us over to the dinner table and does this whole special presentation for us.

"Okay, my wonderful children, I have obtained . . . wait for it . . . wait for it . . ."

"What is it, Mom?" Charlie says, bouncing up and down, hardly able to contain himself.

"So," she says, going through her purse. "I have obtained three tickets to . . ."

"Disney?" Charlie jumps from his seat.

"No, not Disney."

"Ah crap."

"Charles Antonio Vega! Mouth!"

My brother sits and crosses his arms in protest. He's not moving from there for a while.

"We're not going to Disney," my mom continues, "but we are going somewhere. It is . . . Drum roll please . . ."

"You got the tickets to Puerto Rico?" I say, standing up.

She drops the envelope onto the table, a deflated look on her face.

"Way to take the drama out of the surprise, sweetheart."

"It's the only option we ever talked about, Mom."

She livens up again like I didn't just ruin her reveal. "We're going to Puerto Rico!"

"You said that," Charlie says.

"Yes, I did."

"We're staying with Uncle Ermenio?" I ask.

"Yes, we are. And neither the flight nor the stay will cost us any Cookie Monster Cash!"

I look at the ticket again and then at my brother, who is carefully poring over the information on it with me.

"It says Miami on the ticket," Charlie points out.

"We're connecting through Miami and then to San Juan. Cool, huh?"

Charlie studies the itinerary a few more times. "Flight 1836," he says. "We leave Philadelphia at six a.m., arrive in Miami at eight fifty-five a.m., then leave Miami at eleven thirty a.m. and arrive in Puerto Rico at three ten p.m."

"Yep. We're going to be in Puerto Rico for five days. And here's the best part: we leave in two days!"

Charlie jumps up and down like he's just won a million dollars. My mom takes him by the hands and they dance around the table.

Then my mom starts chanting, "My kids and me fly for free! My kids and me fly for free! Well, we pay tax, but still! My kids and me fly free!" I don't dance, but I smile. I definitely smile.

For the next two days, Charlie gets busy checking maps of Puerto Rico and bus routes. I check the weather online and it's eighty degrees in Puerto Rico right now. I can't imagine the end of February being that hot.

I ask my mom if she's talked to Uncle Ermenio about my dad yet, but she keeps avoiding the question. I ask her for my dad's email about a million times. Finally, she gives it to me.

"Remember, this is our vacation."

"But I can still email him," I say. "I mean, we're staying at his uncle's house. He's gotta be in touch with him."

"If your father responds, we'll go see him. Okay?"

I nod.

If I'm being honest, I'm a little excited about the idea of seeing my dad. He hasn't been around, but maybe he's been too shy to reach out. My mom gives me his email. I go to my room and sit at my desk. I turn on my computer and click on the tab to compose a new message. I freeze. How do you start an email to a father you haven't seen in ten years?

Dear Mr. Vega,

Too formal.

Hi,

Hey!

Too excited.

> Yo, what up, Father? It's me, your son
> Marcus.

Nah, that's silly.

> Dear Dad,

No. I keep deleting the email and rewriting. Finally,
I settle on an introduction.

> Hello,

> It's Marcus. Your son. We're going to
> Puerto Rico in a few days. We're staying
> with Uncle Ermenio. Your uncle, my great-
> uncle. You know that. Anyway, if you're
> around, this is my email. I don't know if
> there's Wi-Fi in Puerto Rico. Is there? Well,
> anyway, if you get this before we leave,

I look at the plane ticket.

> maybe you can scoop us up at the
> airport? If you're free. We arrive at 3:10
> p.m. Here's the info.

I type the flight number, the date we arrive, and the
airline we're flying on.

Hopefully you can pick us up. It will be me,
my mom, and Charlie. He's twelve now.
You probably know that. Anyway, this is
my email. I'll be checking it.

Bye,
Marcus

I press send. I refresh a few times and then check
my sent folder to make sure the email went through.
I leave my computer on the rest of the day and check
it whenever I'm in my room to see if he's responded.
My mom doesn't say anything, because she's busy
preparing for the flight. I tell her my dad might pick
us up.

"Okay, sweetheart," she says. "But don't . . ."

"I know," I tell her.

Look, it's completely possible he'll show up. He still
hasn't answered, but that doesn't mean he hasn't read
the email. I make a note to send him another one the
day we leave. To remind him when we arrive. Maybe
he's just busy. He might have the email and decide that
he doesn't need to respond. He'll just show up. I ask my
mom if there's Wi-Fi in Puerto Rico and she says yes
but she doesn't want to be using her phone while we're
there.

I tell her we should bring the phone just in case we
need it.

❖❖❖

The day before we fly, I'm so excited about the trip that I somehow end up at Danny's house. My dad still hasn't emailed back, but it's probably because he hasn't had time to check. I don't know why I end up at Danny's house. I think maybe he would want to hear about the trip.

"Make sure you wear plenty of sunscreen," he says. "It gets very humid in Puerto Rico, and even though it's raining, that doesn't mean you can't get a sunburn."

He tells me about the sustainable farms that are beginning to pop up in parts of the countryside. Danny's a smart kid.

"Take pictures," he says.

"I don't have a camera or a phone with a camera."

He ponders this for a moment. Then his face lights up and he runs into another room in his house.

He comes back and hands me a huge camera case.

"Here you go!"

"I can't take this," I say.

"It's just for a few days," he insists. "And besides, my parents never use it."

"Danny, look, I'm—"

He interrupts before I can finish.

"Listen, this is a once-in-a-lifetime trip. You're going to want to remember it."

I guess he has a point. I'm not used to someone giving me something just because they want to. Usually there is a transaction. I get something, they get something. Fear is generally a factor. This is a first.

I take the camera and thank him. We say good-bye and he offers his hand. I shake it and head back home.

"Hasta luego, Marcus."

"See you," I say, clutching the camera bag.

When I arrive at my house, my mom is pacing up and down the hallway, thinking out loud about all the things we need for the trip.

"Okay, we're going for five days, so that means we need five outfits, one for each day. Or do we need six? Plus extra underwear and shoes. How many pairs of shoes do I need? Oh, I don't need dressy shoes; it's not like I'm going out or anything. . . . And what else?"

"Mom," I say, stepping in front of her. "We're not going away for a month."

I watch her put clothes into one large suitcase and then rush over to my brother's room and come back with another haul. She carefully examines the clothes on her bed.

"We'll take one large suitcase, and each of us will have one carry-on. That way all of our stuff is in one place. Make sense?"

"Mom, we don't need that many clothes."

As my mom digs through her closet, she finds a

box. The look on her face tells me she isn't happy to see it. She makes her way back to the bed and sits down, the box on her lap. I sit next to her as she opens it. She pulls out a few family photos that are folded and wrinkled. There are some movie ticket stubs and letters. Then my mom pulls out my dad's old driver's license. This item seems to suck all the noise out of the air for a moment.

"He just left everything behind," she says. "Then I get a call one day from Puerto Rico. It was your father halfheartedly saying I should join him once he got his new business up and running."

My mom holds the box in her hands. She puts it down and looks at me for a moment before offering a smile.

"And then you wake up and ten years have . . ." My mom trails off. "Do you get why I don't want to see him, sweetheart?" My mom is quiet after she says this.

"But he said to come," I tell her. "And we are; we're going. Maybe it's all just been a huge miscommunication? Maybe he doesn't know what to say. Maybe he thought because you never went that you didn't want to see him."

"Sweetie, I want you to believe that. I really do," she says. "But that's not how these stories end."

I feel the blood rushing to my neck, but I don't say anything. I grab my dad's ID before she can put it away. She may be done with my dad, but I'm not. I want answers.

Charlie hasn't looked up from Mom's laptop the whole time. He's been studying airport maps, flight times, directions to get to Uncle Ermenio's house from the airport, and San Juan's city layout. It doesn't look like he's listening to us, but I bet he is.

My brother is smart. He doesn't remember my dad, but he makes it his mission to learn everything he can about Puerto Rican culture. If he knows everything, he feels prepared. That's really important to him. I came home the other day to some fast Spanish music blasting in my room and Charlie moving his hips like they were connected to supercharged batteries.

"Salsa," he said while he danced.

❀❀❀

I go to my room and grab a few pairs of shorts and shirts and throw them into my backpack. I put aside my good pair of sneakers and lay out a large hoodie and some cargo pants for the plane. I put the camera bag next to my backpack and throw myself onto my bed, thinking about everything.

By the time my mom finishes packing, it's around midnight. Our flight is at six in the morning, and we have to get to the train by three. Charlie is already asleep. I'm not tired, so I stare at the water stains on our ceiling. They spread across the room like mountain ranges. I take my dad's ID out of my pocket.

MARCUS ANTONIO VEGA

My father is about the same height as me. We have the same eyes. Wide brown ovals. We have the same skin that darkens in the sun. Not like my brother. He got my mom's fair complexion. My dad has curly brown hair like mine, only his is longer. And he doesn't smile. Another thing that makes us look exactly alike.

I get up one last time to check my email. He still hasn't responded. I write him another note.

Hi,

I have your ID. Maybe we can meet up when I'm in Puerto Rico? I can give it to you then.

Bye,
Marcus

I look at the note a few times before finally pressing send.

DAY ONE

EIGHT

TRAVEL DAY

Charlie has the same headphones as I do. Except the music coming from his is some kind of salsa music.

"Charlie, it's three thirty in the morning," my mom says. "Turn it down."

He pretends not to hear her. My mom scoots over from her seat on the train to take off his headphones, but he leans away.

"Hey!" he says, clutching them. "My music!"

"Turn it down. You're going to blow out your eardrums."

"No."

My mom doesn't back down. She plucks them off my brother's head in one swift motion. I'm surprised. She usually doesn't confront my brother like that. She usually tries to talk to him first.

"Charlie, I said turn it down. You're going to hurt your ears."

Charlie mumbles something about my mom getting stuck in a tube of chocolate.

"Oh, now I'm Augustus Gloop?" She tickles Charlie to lighten the mood.

Charlie sinks into the train seat as we ride to our connecting bus in Philly. By four thirty we arrive at the airport. Charlie recognizes the stop and tells my mom.

"Thank you, sweetheart," she says. Charlie never stays angry for too long.

There are people already here even though it's so early. There's always somewhere to go, I guess.

"Where are you flying?" asks the airline guy. My mom hands him our huge bag and then our tickets. He checks off my mom's ID and looks at me.

"Your ID, sir?"

"He's my son," my mom says. "He's fourteen."

The guy looks at me like he can't believe what my mom just said. But he returns our tickets and waves us on.

Charlie asks to see his boarding pass and my mom hands it to him.

"Boarding is at five thirty-five. Flight leaves at six o'clock. Gate B sixteen," he says.

We walk to the sliding glass doors, and my mom takes off Charlie's coat and then her own. I leave mine on.

Charlie examines the plane ticket and looks up at the signs.

"We have to go to security check over there," he says, pointing. We take the escalator up, following Charlie's lead. Even though my mom works here, my brother takes pride in knowing where he is. (Like I said, he's been studying the airport layout for days.)

The security guy doesn't make a comment about my size or look at Charlie funny. He just hands my mom her ID back and takes the next person in line. It must be cool to have a job like that. You don't have to make a comment every time you see someone. You just do your job and carry on.

Charlie moves exactly where a security lady directs him. I catch her smiling and winking at Charlie.

Charlie approaches the body scanner and watches the guy in front of him step into the machine and put his hands over his head. The machine makes a whirring sound and Charlie's eyes light up.

"Awesome!"

The guy steps out and continues to walk through security.

"All right, baby," the lady says to Charlie, "your turn."

Charlie puts his hands over his head and smiles

from ear to ear as the machine scans him. I think I even see him bounce a little from excitement.

My mom goes through and then I do. The lady tells us to have a good trip.

We get our carry-on bags off the conveyor belt and head to the gates. I look around, completely shocked. The airport is like its own universe. There are restaurants and shops and sitting areas where people are just waiting to board. Charlie points because he wants to make sure we're at the gate on time.

"We have an hour and a half before our plane leaves, honey," my mom says, but Charlie ignores her and tells us to hurry.

I look at the planes outside, lit by overhead lights. My stomach starts to gurgle, and I feel sweat forming on my forehead.

My mom looks at me. "Are you feeling okay?"

I nod.

"Take off your coat, honey. It's warm in here."

Charlie hurries to our gate.

"B sixteen!" he says, rushing to a window to stare at the plane parked outside. "Look, that's our plane!"

My mom puts our bags across three seats in the waiting area and sits down. Charlie calls me over. I watch other planes taking off in the distance, and I can feel sweat forming on my eyebrows again. My neck starts to itch. I look at Charlie and try to smile.

"Marcus," he says. "You gonna throw up?"

I don't say anything. The floor starts moving slowly from side to side, and I think if I move, I'm going to fall through and break into a million pieces.

My mom brings me a bottle of water that she buys from the newsstand close to our gate. I try not to think about how the water costs four dollars here. Instead I finish it in three gulps and tell her thanks.

"Had me scared for a minute there," she says, feeling my neck.

Even though I'm taller than my mom, it feels nice when she rubs my neck like she did when I was a kid. I don't know what happened just now. I got all dizzy and couldn't move my feet. Weird.

My mom greets a few people working at the gate. They look over at us and smile. Charlie waves and smiles back. I nod.

Eventually, the lady calls out some stuff about boarding first class and military personnel. A guy in army fatigues walks past us, holding a small duffle bag. His name is stitched onto his uniform. R. HERNÁNDEZ. I wonder where he's going after Miami.

Next she calls people with disabilities and people with small children. I see my mom move through the line toward the lady taking tickets. She turns back and motions for us to follow.

Up to now, Charlie has been leading us through the

airport, but he's suddenly stopped and won't leave my side. He looks up and watches me for a minute.

"Come on," he says, and takes my hand.

We get to my mom and she introduces us to her coworkers.

"This is Marcus and Charlie," my mom says to the lady.

"Oh my, what gorgeous boys, Mel. Hi, boys! My name is Margie. This is Rhonda. And that grumpy fellow over there is Steve."

"I'm not grumpy!" Steve says as he makes an exaggerated grumpy face.

Charlie cracks up. "He's grumpy!"

"About time you took those boys on a trip," Rhonda says.

"Yeah," my mom says, looking at us, then back at Rhonda.

"You boys have a great flight, okay?" says Margie.

"Take care of your momma," Steve says, patting Charlie on the back.

I nod. They all seem nice. We walk inside this cave-like tunnel, and my head starts spinning again. It feels like I'm going to get trapped in here with whatever little oxygen there is.

"Marcus, take off your coat. It's too hot."

We shuffle closer and closer to the plane. Charlie notices my sweating.

"Hey, man," he says, "don't freak out."

"I won't," I tell him.

My brother, the motivational speaker.

I try not to think too hard about where I am, and focus more on where we're going. I think of what it will be like in Puerto Rico. There are lots of beaches and old forts from what I read online. The ocean surrounding Puerto Rico looks like it's made of blue crystals. I've been to lakes and stuff in the summer, but nothing that has those bright colors.

When we finally get to the plane, it has a stale kind of smell to it. Like a mixture of freshly brewed coffee and leftover sandwiches. There is a quiet hum inside, and a guy in a blue suit greets us as we make our way inside.

"Well, hello," the guy says to Charlie. "Hi, Mel!"

"Hi, Sam," she replies.

Sam takes something out of a metal drawer and hands it to Charlie.

"This is for our honorary pilots," he says. It's a tiny airplane pin.

Charlie smiles.

"Say thank you to Sam, sweetheart," my mom says.

"Thank you, Sam."

My mom pins the little airplane to Charlie's shirt. Then he turns to me.

"I'm captain. You obey me."

"Yeah, right," I tell him. "Come on, Captain. Get your butt to your seat."

We're toward the middle, by the wing. I can't believe the huge airplane I saw through the window feels so tiny inside. I can barely walk down the aisle. We wait while a guy takes off his suit jacket and hangs it in a closet by his seat. His seat is gray and seems bigger and shinier than the ones in the back, which are blue and don't look as comfortable.

My mom looks at the top of the aisles for our seat number.

"Here we are," she says. "Seats twenty A, B, and C. Marcus, you take the aisle because your legs are longer. And take off your coat!"

I help put our bags in the overhead compartment. I make sure my backpack is secure, because I have Danny's camera in it. Why did I agree to bring it? I close the overhead bin and finally sit down. These seats are way too small. My mom takes the middle so Charlie can watch the plane take off from the window. She takes both of our hands in hers. People start filling in the other seats.

After a few announcements and some safety video about what to do if the plane crashes into the ocean, the pilot asks the crew to get ready for takeoff. The plane chugs along while Charlie keeps pointing at the other planes going airborne. I start sweating again. I want him to stop calling that out. I close my eyes, but my head spins faster.

Here I am, big, bad Marcus Vega, totally afraid of flying.

The engines roar to life and the plane skips and then breaks into a sprint. The whole cabin rumbles and shakes and my head sinks back into the little blue headrest. I close my eyes again.

"Marcus, you are going to faint if you don't take off your coat."

I start pulling at my sleeves. My arm stretches across the aisle and accidentally bumps someone.

"Sorry," I say. It was the soldier from before.

"No worries," he says, pulling the coat to help me get my arm out.

"Thanks," I say.

My mom squeezes my hand and puts her head on my shoulder. Then she kisses Charlie on the forehead. I open my eyes for a second and see her watching us both as the plane rises higher and higher into the clouds. I peek out the window. The buildings and houses look like toys you could pick up between two fingers. I glance at my mom, then out the window again. The city gets more and more distant. She looks back and smiles.

"Go team go," she says.

NINE
LAYOVER AND TOUCHDOWN

A dinging sound rings throughout the plane as it levels off. The captain says something about "cruising altitude" and tells us how long the flight will be. We're in the air, and I alternate between closing my eyes and opening them. Neither makes me feel better. My mom reaches over and rubs my neck.

In a few hours, we'll land. Will my dad pick us up at the Puerto Rico airport? Will he be happy we came all this way to see him? What's he gonna say when he sees Charlie? My mom seems excited. She keeps repeating that this is a much-needed adventure with her boys.

"We're going to have so much fun," she says.

"You think he's going to be there?"

"He's somewhere. . . ." she says.

●●●

About three hours pass when the captain makes an announcement.

"We have begun our descent into Miami International Airport. Flight attendants, prepare for landing."

The flight attendants move quickly down the aisle to make sure people are buckled in and their seats are pushed up. I have to move my leg back into our row, and my knees shove the seat in front of me. It is so cramped. I feel like someone has tied my legs together in a sitting position.

As the plane starts to drop, my ears hum and pop. I look over and see Charlie shaking his head and opening his mouth. My mom takes out a pack of gum and hands a piece to each of us.

"Chew it—it'll help with your ears."

He looks over and motions with his mouth.

"My ears will explode."

"They're not going to explode, Charlie," she says. "Big exaggerator."

The buildings in the distance start to get bigger, and I can see the ocean touching the edges of the land. It's like looking at the edges of my mom's eyes. The water is a deep green outlined by dark brown patches of land. The plane is going so fast and the buildings zip by us. How is the pilot going to land this thing?

There is a screech and a thump as our wheels meet the runway. The plane jolts forward, and my knees almost rip through the seat in front of me. The impact sends my head forward a little, and I feel my mom's hands squeeze mine. Suddenly, we slow and settle into a glide.

I can't believe we have to do all of this one more time before we get to Puerto Rico.

❀❀❀

On our second flight, I feel much calmer. I even concentrate long enough to skim some of the books Charlie picked up at the airport.

"Why did you get this?" I ask, pointing to the copy of *Proud to Be Boricua* in his hands.

"I like it," he responds, tapping on the cover. The cover features a guy proudly holding the flag of the United States in one hand and what must be the Puerto Rican flag in the other. I ask to borrow it and read the first few lines.

I am Puerto Rican. I am an American citizen. What is my home? Where do I belong?

I read a few more lines.

. . . I understand both worlds because they exist in the same person . . .

The author writes that he is a Boricua living in the United States. He says he lives in a small town in the States but spends his summers in a town called Culebra in Puerto Rico.

All this talk about two stories makes me think of my dad. Is this how he feels? I was born in Puerto Rico, but Springfield definitely feels like my home. I'll add this to the questions I want to ask him.

I switch to *A Traveler's Guide to Puerto Rico* to learn more about where we're staying. There are tons of photographs and descriptions of places. San Juan is the capital, and Old San Juan is a neighborhood where most travelers stay because "it features colorful Spanish colonial buildings, street-side cafés, shops, nightclubs, and el Morro and la Fortaleza, two massive centuries-old fortresses." I look at the map of Puerto Rico. There are millions of people living on the island. My dad is out there somewhere.

After a few hours, we finally start our descent. We drop farther and farther, and a tower and the ocean come into focus. Then I don't see anything but the gray of the runway. Is something wrong? I close my eyes, hoping the plane isn't going to skid off into the ocean. So much for being less stressed. Clearly, I have a flying-in-the-sky-inside-a-tin-can issue. The plane touches down and slows to a roll on the tarmac.

The captain welcomes us to San Juan. Outside the window, I see a grassy knoll with several words scrolled over it: AEROPUERTO INTERNACIONAL LUIS MUÑOZ MARÍN.

"We need to find baggage claim," my mom says as we wait to get off the plane, "and then a taxi to Ermenio's place."

My mom leads the way this time. Charlie and I look around the airport as we follow. There's a barbershop, a souvenir shop, something that looks like a clothing store, a food market, a McDonald's. Are all airports supposed to look like malls?

I see a sign above us.

RECLAMO DE EQUIPAJE

"It says baggage claim over there," I say, eyeing the translation underneath.

Everywhere we look there are signs in Spanish with the English translation right below. We go down an escalator and reach an area that looks like a park. There are benches and some trees and what looks like a row of little houses. I see another baggage claim sign around the corner and point. Charlie moves ahead past the little park-like area and stops to show us where the bags from our flight will be.

"It's here," he says.

My mom's huge bag eventually shoots out and lands on the carousel. We take it and walk to the sliding doors. When they open, the heat washes over me and it hits me that I'm somewhere completely different.

I check my mom's phone and sign in to my email to see if maybe my dad has responded. He hasn't yet. As my mom hails a cab, I write him another email.

Hi,

It's me. Marcus. Letting you know that we landed. Figure you're busy. We're just going to take a cab to Uncle Ermenio's house. You probably know the address. We'll be there for a few days.

Bye,
Marcus

I press send and shove the phone into my pocket. Mom says she wants to unplug on vacation, so I can hang on to it. I look around and spot the one sign that doesn't have an English translation: ¡BIENVENIDOS!

I don't speak Spanish, but I know that means "welcome."

TEN

OLD SAN JUAN HAS WI-FI

We hop in a taxi, and the first thing the driver does is turn down his music. My mom tries her best Spanish, but the guy responds in English before she can finish.

"I'll get you to Viejo San Juan in about, eh, a little over twenty minutes."

The guy taps his steering wheel to quiet music as we head down the highway. I see a line of little flags that stretch about a mile long. There are US flags and a Puerto Rican flag with a sideways triangle and one star in it, like in the book I looked at.

I read that Puerto Rico is part of the United States, but right now it feels like we're in a totally different country. The buildings are old-looking. Some are painted white or really bright shades of pink, blue, and even lime green. It looks nothing like my neighborhood back home. I can see the outlines of the ocean from our window. Charlie rolls it down and puts his hand out. The air whips in and the sound of the city fills the taxi. This city sounds like honking, music, and fast cars and trucks zooming by us on their way to places I don't know.

"What do you have planned on our beautiful island?" the driver asks.

My mom says we're staying for a few days.

"Then you have to check out las playas en Manatí and make sure to visit el Morro."

My brother tells him we're on vacation and looking for our dad.

"¿Qué dijo? I don't understand what he said."

The driver asks Charlie to repeat himself a few more times. He doesn't understand him. Charlie huffs, and I can tell he's getting irritated that he's being misunderstood. It happens to him when someone doesn't know him.

"He's saying we're going to find our dad," I tell the guy, because I'm getting irritated also.

The driver adjusts the rearview mirror, and I can see he's focused on Charlie.

"Okay, sorry, I didn't understand him too good. My fault."

He's quiet the rest of the ride and I'm glad. He was talking too much.

We cross over a bridge and I get a full view of the ocean. There is a harbor and a large cruise ship just pulling in. It makes everything in the water around it look tiny. It reminds me of school. That's what I am at Montgomery. A cruise ship surrounded by tiny boats in the ocean called middle school.

Snap. I take a picture with Danny's camera. I might as well, since I have it.

A sign coming up says VIEJO SAN JUAN. That means "Old San Juan." It does look old. I start thinking I know more Spanish than I thought, because I've translated more words in the last hour than I did all last year in Spanish class.

Old San Juan has buildings that look like they were constructed hundreds of years ago. *Snap*. We drive through tiny streets that our taxi barely squeezes through. *Snap*.

It feels nice disappearing behind the lens. It's like looking without being looked at. And when you're my size, you're always looked at.

The driver zigs, zags, and honks when he wants someone to get out of his way. My mom looks at the street signs while Charlie tracks our progress on the map in his lap. I just watch all the restaurants and coffee shops and bars lining the tiny sidewalks. *Snap*. *Snap*. *Snap*. My mom smiles. *Snap*.

The driver finally pulls over, practically running over someone on the sidewalk. He yanks the emergency break and the lever that pops open the trunk before he hops out. He struggles with our huge suitcase, so I help.

My mom pays the driver and he hops back in his car and zips off.

Charlie looks at the building in front of us.

"What the heck is that?"

"That's Uncle Ermenio's place," my mom says, half-smiling. "It's cozy."

"It says 'hostel,' Mom." Charlie points at the creaky old sign above the green double door. "Do we need medicine?"

My mom shakes her head. "No, sweetie, a hostel is an affordable place to stay when you travel."

"You just said it was Uncle Ermenio's house, though." I'm confused.

"It is. He owns this building and runs it as a hostel. We're sleeping in this adorable little bungalow on the roof."

My brother and I look at each other.

"What?" we both say.

"I used to stay here with your father. It's super fun and the price is right—free!"

If my mom is trying to convince us that this building that looks like it's about to crumble is going to be "super fun," she's officially lost her mind.

I snap a few pictures anyway. "Mom," I say, "there aren't any doorknobs. The window is literally made of plastic bags and tape."

"Oh, so you go from being a tough guy to suddenly being precious about windows? It has character!"

The building looks more like something out of a horror movie. And did I hear correctly? She says we're staying on the roof?

"Mom, the building looks too old."

"Where's your sense of adventure?"

Charlie turns back to the street. "Where is the taxi?"

"Come on, you two. I'm not raising a bunch of chickens."

My mom leads the way. We approach carefully behind her as she opens the creaky door. *Snap.* Sunlight enters the room, but it only creates a sharp beam that barely illuminates anything but the tip of the staircase. *Snap.* My mom walks in, and I wonder if we should wait to be invited inside first. *Snap. Snap. Snap.*

Mom turns back and smiles as I let the camera dangle around my neck and take Charlie's hand. When Mom faces the stairs again, someone is standing right in front of her.

"Melissa!"

Charlie lets out a noise like he just got the air punched out of him. Which is less embarrassing than what I do (say "Ah!" and swat the air in front of me). My mom smiles once she recognizes who it is.

"Ermenio!" she says, bringing him into a hug.

"Pero mi vida ¡qué flaquita estás!" he says, looking my mom up and down. "¡No estás comiendo!"

My mom smiles shyly, then looks at us. "He always says I need to eat more."

"¿Y estos hombrecitos?"

"Marcus y Charlie," my mom says.

"Hola, mis queridos. ¿Cómo están?"

Charlie and I look at each other, then at Uncle Ermenio.

"Sorry, we don't speak Spanish," I say.

Uncle Ermenio looks at us carefully. He's wearing a suit and tie. His hair is perfectly slicked back and he is sporting the puffiest mustache I have ever seen.

"Ah," he says, then looks at my mom. "Hay que hablarle en español, Melissa. Qué pérdida."

"You're right," she says. "I *should* speak to them more in Spanish, Uncle Ermenio." My mom has a guilty look on her face.

"Pero ¿qué es ese 'Uncle'? ¡Soy Tío! Tío Ermenio," he says, telling us to call him tío instead of uncle.

"Está bien, Tío," Mom agrees.

"Since when do you speak Spanish, Mom?" I ask, totally confused.

"I minored in Spanish in college, sweetheart. I did a

semester here. It's where I met your dad . . . You know this!"

"Nope," I say, because I really don't. I knew my mom met my dad in Puerto Rico, but I never knew she spoke so much Spanish.

Uncle Ermenio gives me a hug and then kisses my cheek. I step back because I've never been kissed on the cheek like that before.

"Umm, thanks, Mr. Tío Ermenio," I say.

"Just tío," he says, then turns back to my mom. "Ay, Melissa. Pero ¿cómo va pasar tanto tiempo sin ver estos niños?" He takes Charlie's hand and then mine and holds us close.

"Perdón, Tío," my mom says. "I just, you know, Marcus, and . . ." My mom is trying to get words out. She's talking about my dad, not me.

"Yo sé, mi amor," Uncle Ermenio says, kissing her cheek and rubbing her shoulder.

"Bueno," he continues. "Están aquí ahora, y eso es lo importante."

My mom smiles. Charlie and I look at her.

"Care to translate?" I ask, because we're totally lost.

My mom says Uncle Ermenio is sad that we haven't visited him since my parents split up. She told him she hasn't spoken to my dad in a long time.

"But he said what's important is that we're here

now," my mom says. I can tell she feels guilty about not coming sooner. Her eyes get droopy and glassy when she feels bad about something.

Tío Ermenio holds his hip and starts limping a little. My mom asks him if he's okay. He starts in Spanish, then switches to English.

"Bad hip," he says. "Pero imagine, the wait to get a doctor's appointment . . ." Tío Ermenio trails off. "Many doctors on the island have left to the States for better reimbursements from insura—" He stops, leans against the stairs, and rubs his side. "No pasa nada," he says. "It's okay."

"You're limping pretty bad, Tío," my mom says.

"Nah, está bien. Bueno," he says, clapping and smiling again. "Let me show the boys around."

He takes us through the living room, where there are books stacked high in several corners. They lean awkwardly and look like they might topple over at any minute. I see a few photographs on the mantelpiece. There is one of a younger Tío Ermenio holding hands with a lady. There's another one with him and a whole bunch of kids on a farm.

"Este flaco aquí is your father," he says, pointing to a tall skinny kid in the picture.

"What's he doing?" I ask.

"That's the farm of my late wife's sister, Darma."

He tells me that my dad used to love going there.

"He had a connection to the land. He loved farming and riding horses."

My dad is wearing a cowboy hat and a tank top. He's smiling. He looks happy. I wouldn't know why, because I've never seen a horse up close before.

"How old was he there?" I ask.

"Eh, creo que he was about thirteen en esta foto," he explains. "And these are all his cousins. They're your cousins once removed."

I never knew I had cousins.

"Only they're grown-up now. Actually, this one here is Sergio." Tío Ermenio points to another kid standing close to my dad. "He's staying here with his daughter, María, and two of her best friends. You'll meet them!"

"I remember that farm," my mom suddenly says. "How is Darma?"

"She's good," Tío Ermenio replies. "Stubborn as always. But good. You should go see her while you're here."

"That would be nice," Mom says. "My gosh, that farm was beautiful."

My mom never talks about my Puerto Rican family. I always figured it was because she didn't know too much about them. But now it seems like she knows more than I thought. I don't get it. Why wouldn't she say anything back home?

"We'll call her," Tío Ermenio says. "If she decides to

answer her phone. Esa mujer always refuses to answer the phone. She likes to be, ¿cómo se dice? Off the grid."

Tío Ermenio heads into the kitchen. We follow him and he tells us to sit at the counter while he prepares a snack.

"We're okay, Tío," my mom says. "We had lunch on our layover in Miami."

"I'm not going to let you go hungry!"

"We're really not that—"

Tío Ermenio doesn't let my mom finish. He takes out two pieces of something that looks like it got run over by a car. It's completely flattened. Then he takes out mayonnaise that smells like garlic and starts slicing a tomato. When he's finished, he carefully layers some meat on the table.

"Oh my gosh," my mom says excitedly. "Jibarito!"

"Aha," Tío Ermenio says while my mom moves around the counter to help.

"A what?" Charlie says.

"Hee-bah-ree-toh." My mom breaks it down phonetically for Charlie. "It's a fried plantain sandwich with garlic mayonnaise, tomato, onions. Oh my gosh!"

"What's that?" Charlie says. He gives the sandwich a strange look.

"It has a good story," Tío Ermenio says. "The original jibarito sandwich was created in Chicago by a Puerto Rican named Juan Figueroa. It wasn't a traditional

Puerto Rican sandwich, but he made something new and original with it. Now it's very popular."

"How many Puerto Ricans live in Chicago?" I ask.

"There are more Puertorriqueños in the United States than actually live on the island," he says.

"Wow," Charlie says, helping himself to the sandwich. He takes a bite, and the tomato slips out of the plantain, but he scoops it up with his hand and shoves it into his mouth.

"Whoa, careful there, man," I tell him. "You're going to choke."

I take a bite of my sandwich. It is pretty delicious.

"After you're finished, let's go and see if the others are awake."

"Is there Wi-Fi here?" I ask.

"Oh yes," he says. "Sometimes the rain makes it bad, but mostly it's pretty good."

I ask him for the password. He digs into a drawer and pulls out a whole bunch of papers. He skims through them, looking for the password.

"I keep telling myself to write all these passwords down in one place," he says, scattering papers everywhere.

My mom comes around the counter and watches me carefully. "What do you need Wi-Fi for?" she asks.

"I dunno," I tell her, trying to avoid an explanation. My mom doesn't press the issue. She leaves the kitchen and follows Charlie, who is already checking out the rest of the place. Finally, Tío Ermenio pulls out a paper with the password.

"¡Aquí está!" he declares, handing it to me. I type the information into my mom's phone and wait for a connection.

"Thanks," I say.

Tío Ermenio leaves the kitchen to meet my mom and Charlie by the stairs.

"I'll be right there," I say, quickly checking my email.

My dad hasn't responded.

I start typing.

Hi,

We got to Tio Ermenio's house.

Pretty cool here. He made us a

I look around to see how to spell the name of the sandwich. Finally, I yell out to my mom.

"*J-i-b-a-r-i-t-o!*" she yells back.

jibarito. It was good. Anyway, we're here for a couple of days. I already told you that.

Okay, bye,
Marcus

"Marcus, honey, let's go upstairs." My mom walks
into the kitchen. "Are you on the phone?"

I press send and put the phone away. "Nah, I was
just checking something."

She eyes me, but I push past her and head to the
stairs.

"Let's check out the rest of the place," I tell her before she starts asking more questions.

ELEVEN

RELATIVE DISTANCE

I look at a framed photograph of my dad on a mantel by the stairs. He's older in this one.

"When's the last time you saw my dad?" I ask.

Tío Ermenio shakes his head. "I haven't seen him in about a year. He was helping me with the hostel, and then one day he wanted to turn my house into a technology . . . something. I don't know. He got angry and left when I said no."

"Where did he go?" I ask.

"Honey, we just got here," my mom says, sounding annoyed. "Can we at least unpack before we get into all of this?"

"I just want to know how far away he might be."

My mom sighs.

"Your father . . ." Tío Ermenio starts. "Well, he always has a new 'project.'"

"Where do you think he went?" I ask.

"That's enough dad sleuthing for today," my mom says, rolling our suitcase to the stairs. "I want to explore the neighborhood!"

Tío Ermenio takes the suitcase. He looks back and smiles at us. I remove the cap from Danny's camera and aim. *Snap.*

"Síguenme," he says, motioning for us to follow him up the stairs. "It's a few flights up. No elevator. Sorry."

Charlie doesn't say anything, but I know he's scared by the way he keeps looking around the corners of the other rooms as we reach the top of each flight. My mom is already halfway up the second flight as Ermenio walks along the second floor. He knocks lightly and waits a moment.

"Ja bitte?" a girl says from inside.

"Hello, Hilda? Angela? I want to introduce you to my family." Tío Ermenio politely waits by the door. "These are María's very good friends. They met two summers ago when María did a high school foreign exchange program in Berlin. That girl has tremendous ambitions. All three of them."

Tío Ermenio tries to tell us what María and her

friends want to study in college, but he can't seem to find the right word in English.

"¡Dímelo en español!" my mom says.

I still can't get over the fact that she knows so much Spanish. Tío Ermenio says a few things while Mom carefully pays attention. When he's done, she turns to us and translates what he said.

"Tío says María wants to study agricultural engineering; her friend from Berlin, Angela, is studying biochemistry at a university in Berlin; and Angela's twin sister, Hilda . . ."

"Hallo, Tío Ermenio!" A tall girl with bright red hair who's older than me opens the door.

"Hilda is undecided," Mom says.

"She's such a kind girl," Tío Ermenio offers.

Hilda gives Tío Ermenio a kiss on the cheek.

"Hello, Hilda," he says. "Meine, em . . . My German isn't very good," he says to us. "This is mi familia. Melissa, Marcus Jr., y Charlie."

"Schön, euch kennenzulernen," Hilda says. I think she's going to speak more German, but she switches easily to English. "It's lovely to meet you all! Ermenio has been talking about your visit for days."

My mom says hello and I wave. Charlie can't stop staring.

"Hallo, handsome sir. And what is your name?"

"Charlie," he says, acting all shy.

"Charlie," she says, "it is wonderful to make your acquaintance."

"I have a Wonka hat," he says digging into his backpack.

"Oh," she says.

Charlie pulls out a totally flattened hat, and his shoulders sag a little. He starts mumbling about his too-small backpack and the cramped plane and the whole trip in general.

"Hey," Hilda says. "Can I see?"

Charlie looks at his hat and pulls it in close. The hat is bent and twisted. He leans into my mom. My mom tries to help, but he just keeps the hat close and doesn't talk.

"Maybe we'll fix it later?" Hilda says to Charlie. Charlie doesn't respond.

"Hallo!" says another girl, popping up behind Hilda. She looks identical to Hilda, except she has really curly blonde hair. "Wer ist das? Oh, Ermenio, this is your family from the US?"

"Sí! I mean, ja!"

The girl waves. "Hallo, I'm Angela."

"They're on a break from school," Tío Ermenio says.

"Hilda's always on a break," Angela says, smirking.

"Really?" Hilda replies. "Well, at least I know how to have fun."

"I have fun," Angela says with a huff. "Just not *all* the time."

"You should have just told Papa you didn't want to come," Hilda says.

"Ja klar," Angela says. "As if he would let us separate."

The sisters stare at each other for a minute, and it looks like they're about to get into a fight. Hilda playfully shoves her sister and her sister does the same.

"Das stimmt," Hilda agrees. "Very, very true."

"Our father likes us being together wherever we go," Angela says. "He says we look out for each other. But I think, maybe most of the time, I'm looking out for Hilda."

Hilda scoffs and crosses her arms. I think they're mad again, but they end up laughing.

"Good-bye, my good man," Hilda says to Charlie. "See you soon?"

Charlie finally looks up. I can tell he's thinking about smiling.

We walk up another flight of stairs, and Ermenio shakes his head at a door marked 3F.

"This is where your father was staying. After our disagreement, he just stormed off. Left his bags, everything. Never returned."

"Imagine that," my mom says, not even looking at the room.

"This way is the common bathroom—"

"I'm so sorry I haven't been better about visiting, Tío Ermenio," my mom interrupts. Her eyes get droopy again and she sighs a few times.

"Pero no te preocupes por eso, mi amor," Tío Ermenio replies. "You are here now. With your boys. This is good."

My mom nods, and it looks like she's trying not to let her glossy eyes turn into tears.

Tío Ermenio pauses and appears to get lost in his thoughts before he takes off again up another flight of stairs. I hear him mumbling something about "niño" and something else about "su familia," but like I said, I don't speak Spanish.

We go up a fifth flight, and Charlie starts to complain. He says he doesn't want to go up any more stairs. I can tell he's not comfortable. He starts talking about going home.

"We're almost there, sweetie," my mom says, climbing another flight of stairs.

Tío Ermenio stops and walks down to my brother. "You know, you look like an adventurer."

My brother isn't paying attention. He's sick of walking. Honestly, I don't blame him. This place stinks like rotting wood, and the floorboards creak like they are going to crack open under us. I can hear water running, and then a man yells out, "¡Hija! Wait till I'm done using the toilet!"

An older girl walks out in a bathrobe and waits impatiently in the hall.

"Hola, María," Tío Ermenio says.

"Hola, Tío." She starts talking Spanish so fast, I can barely make out a word.

Tío Ermenio tells her something that sounds like he's trying to calm her down before he introduces us in English.

"This is your family, María. All the way from Pennsylvania, USA!"

"¿Qué tal?" she says, then yells, "¡Papi, apurate! ¡Me estoy congelando!"

"When someone uses the bathroom," Tío Ermenio says calmly, "the shower turns very cold. You'll be fine, though. The shower upstairs is outdoors, so it never feels too cold."

"My goodness, María, you're all grown-up! You're beautiful," my mom says.

María nods and says thank you.

"Do you remember Melissa?" Tío Ermenio asks.

"No, not really," María says. "Sorry."

"I wouldn't think you would. You were six or seven years old," my mom says. "I remember you loved eating fish and veggies on the porch of your tía Darma's farm. It was the cutest thing."

"She did!" Tío Ermenio confirms. There's an awkward pause. María looks around as though she's wondering if she should stay or not.

"It's nice to see you," she finally says before heading to her room.

"María and her father, Sergio, come down to sell produce at the farmers' market on the weekends," Tío Ermenio says. "Sergio says it's the only time he gets to spend with his daughter anymore. She's leaving in the fall to start school in Florida. He's very emotional about it. Don't bring it up."

"So the farmers' market is still around?" Mom asks.

"It's even bigger now!" Tío Ermenio says. "All local products crecido en Puerto Rico!" He raises his hands excitedly, then loses his balance a little. He holds on to the stair railing. "Esta bendita cadera." He rubs his hip. "I'll get it replaced eventually."

María steps out of her room. "Me voy a resfriar," María says, shivering. "¡Papi!"

"¡Ya voy!" yells a voice from the shared bathroom. "Dios mío, los teenagers no tienen paciencia pa'nada."

We all look at Tío Ermenio.

"They love each other," he says, and keeps walking up another flight of stairs.

I ask my mom what they were saying. She tells me that María was yelling at her dad because she was cold and didn't have hot water to shower. Her dad was yelling that his teenage daughter doesn't have any patience. I don't understand any of it.

The toilet flushes, and the sound of water trickling down through the building breaks the quiet.

"Okay, hija. ¡Bañate!"

"¡Gracias!" María runs into the other bathroom. A guy peeks his head up at us from the third floor.

"Mel? You've arrived!"

"Hola, Sergio," my mom says.

"Good flight?"

"Yeah, it was fine. No delays, thank goodness."

Sergio. This was the guy from the photos who Tío Ermenio said is one of my dad's cousins.

"Your boys are so big," he says. "You know, I knew you when you were this small." Sergio puts his arms together like he's cradling an imaginary baby. "You're tall como tu papá."

"My dad?"

"Yeah," Sergio says. "Although I think you got him beat."

Sergio walks over to us and puts his hand on Charlie's shoulder. "And this must be Charlie," he says.

Charlie watches Sergio for a moment. "Hi," he says quietly.

"I saw many pictures of you as a baby. Did you know that?"

Charlie nods.

"You did? What a memory!"

Charlie smiles.

"Hey, I'm taking the girls to the lawn by el Morro tonight if you all want to go. There'll be fireworks and music."

Charlie's ears perk up. "I love fireworks, Marcus," he whispers.

"I know, man."

"Fun!" my mom chimes in.

"I want to go," Charlie says.

"Let's get up to the room first," I tell him. "Cool?"

Charlie nods and immediately starts climbing stairs. I guess he isn't tired anymore. Tío Ermenio watches me.

"You're a good brother," he says, and pats my arm.

We finally get to a door at the top of the final flight of stairs. Tío Ermenio unlocks it and steps through.

My mom and Charlie pause, and when I get to them, I see why they haven't walked any farther. There is a long suspension bridge that runs above the rooftop area to a terrace. On the terrace, there's something that looks like a miniature house. I can see the ocean peeking through the other rooftops from where I'm standing.

"Oh, I remember the bridge!" my mom exclaims. "So much fun."

"What is that?" I ask.

"My late wife, your tía abuela, and I thought it would be fun for the kids to cross a bridge to get to us," Tío

Ermenio explains. "There are also stairs over there."

Charlie and I look at each other. No more stairs.

"So," I ask, watching the suspension bridge. "You had kids?"

"No, we never had kids of our own. A long time ago my Milagro and I turned our home into a hostel. And it has come in handy to accommodate so many nieces and nephews. We used to live up here, but I've moved to the bottom floor because of my hip."

Tío Ermenio points to the tiny house on the terrace. "That will be your place."

My mom offers us a smile that looks a lot like an apology. "See, guys? An adventure bridge."

My mom starts walking across the bridge, and it sways side to side.

Charlie tugs at my shirt. "I want to see the fireworks."

"Not now, man. I'm trying to figure out if that thing will hold me."

Tío Ermenio and my mom cross and wave us over. Charlie tiptoes across while holding the rope railing.

"Be careful, man," I tell him as the bridge starts to look more like a swing.

He gives a thumbs-up and starts waving for me to hurry. "Go fast. I want to see fireworks," he says. He pauses for a second and adds, "You might be too big!"

"Wait till I get over there," I tell him.

"I promise you," Tío Ermenio says. "It is completely safe."

I walk to the edge and put my foot on one of the planks. It feels like I'm trying to balance on a skateboard.

"Can't we just stay in a room downstairs?" I say, because honestly, I don't think this bridge will support my weight. I should have just taken one more flight of stairs.

"Don't be a chicken," my brother says. He starts gobbling like a fool with feathers.

"Come on, sweetie," my mom says.

I take another step and then another. I'm entirely on the bridge, trying not to move too much. I make the mistake of looking down to see that the rooftop is far enough that, if I slip, I'm going to bust my butt. I close my eyes and hurry across.

"Finally!" my brother says, shaking his head. "Took *forever*."

"Pipe down, funny guy," I tell him. "I'm not big on heights."

Charlie laughs uncontrollably and then hugs me. He takes my neck and brings me down to his face. "Nose kiss," he says, wiggling his nose across mine.

He's done that since he was little.

I take his head in my armpit and rub his hair with my knuckle.

"So you got jokes, huh? Huh?"

He cracks up.

My mom and Tío Ermenio head toward the shack. Charlie and I follow, and when we get there, Tío shows my mom the outdoor shower.

"This is the only private shower in the building," he says.

What's private about an outdoor shower on a rooftop surrounded by buildings? Tío Ermenio draws the curtain and twists the shower knobs. Water makes the shower rumble to life.

"It's a little cool, but in this heat it's refreshing."

He opens the door to the small house and lets us in. On one side, there is a double bed covered with a net, and a twin in the corner. On the other side, there's a small stove and a refrigerator that looks more like a box, and a closet that is barely the size of my mom's suitcase. A wooden desk and chair rest below a window that has a view down to the rooftop area. This place isn't just small. It's a dollhouse. I feel like I stepped off a beanstalk. My head barely misses the creaky fan that twirls above.

"It's small," Tío Ermenio says.

The understatement of the millennium.

"But my Milagro and I only stayed in here to sleep. Most of the time we were out on the rooftop with all the kids."

"Tía Milagro was a wonderful person," my mom offers. "I wish I could have been here for the funeral."

"You need to stop making yourself feel guilty about everything, Melissa," Tío Ermenio says. "Guilt does nothing for the spirit."

He hands us the keys and tells us that the whole rooftop is ours to use as we wish. "I will bring fresh café con leche in the morning con bocadillos de guava."

"Thank you," my mom says as Tío Ermenio leaves. She rushes over to him and gives him a long hug.

"I'm glad you're here, mi amor." He holds her face as he says this. "Okay, I'll see you in a little while!" Tío Ermenio crosses the bridge expertly and heads back downstairs.

"Well, team?" my mom says. "Ready to explore?"

"I want to see fireworks," Charlie says.

"I think that's a great idea," Mom replies, throwing herself on the bed. She's smiling. Something about the way she exhales sounds like she's happy she's in this tiny shack in this ancient neighborhood with a bunch of my dad's relatives. My mom wants to relax. My brother wants to see fireworks.

I want more answers.

TWELVE

FIREWORKS

My mom loves the outdoor shower.

"I feel so free out here!"

Charlie is dressed and ready to see the fireworks. My mom gets dressed and we head down from our rooftop in the middle of Old San Juan. I take Danny's camera and pull it over my neck. It's heavy, but there's something comforting about the way it weighs down and rests against my chest. Like it's a shield or something. A shield I can lift up and hide behind whenever I want. We cross the bridge, and this time I don't look down. It doesn't sway as much as before. The first person we see downstairs is Sergio.

"Hey!" he says, offering his hand. "Ready to see the fireworks?"

"Yes," Charlie says.

"You know," Sergio says, "I love fireworks."

Charlie smiles. "Me too."

"Well, we don't want to miss the show. Shall we go?"

"Yes," my mom says, taking Charlie and me by the hand. She looks at me. "Adventure, huh, sweetie?"

"Yeah," I say as we get to my dad's old room. I stop in front of it. "Hey, um, Sergio?"

"What's up?"

"Have you, um, have you . . ."

"Your father and I, we used to be very close. He was a great farmer," Sergio says. "But he went his way and I went mine."

"Where did he go?"

"He had big plans for an agritourism business, but it didn't work out."

"Have you spoken to him?"

"Not for a while. Last time we saw each other was a few years ago. Maybe longer. He wanted to talk to Darma, but she became very upset at him."

"What happened?"

"Why don't we talk about this later? We don't want to miss the show, do we?"

I shake my head. But I still want to find a way to get into my dad's old room. How hard can it be to push in the door? We find the two German girls, Angela and Hilda, at the bottom of the stairs, waiting by the door.

"Fireworks!" Hilda says to Charlie.

María is the next to join us. She smiles at Charlie when she sees him.

"Buenas noches, lindo," she says, rubbing his shoulder. Charlie soaks in every bit of María's affection.

"He's a flirt!" she says as Charlie gets all googly-eyed.

María goes outside with Angela and Hilda. My mom, Charlie, and I follow, while Sergio goes to close the door with no knobs. Tío Ermenio emerges before he can.

"I have to stay here at the front desk. Have a good time, children," he says.

"We will, Ermenio," Sergio says, walking with the rest of us. "Tío doesn't really have anybody checking into the hostel anymore," he adds, out of earshot. "But I think part of him likes to keep watch in case somebody does come."

"Tío is always home," María says suddenly. "He likes to keep watch over the house in case anybody needs a bed to sleep in."

"Very true," Sergio says. "All the tías and tíos in our family are like that."

There's something comforting about that, I guess. Like it makes it feel less lonely or something. Everyone says good-bye, and Tío Ermenio continues to wave at us from the stoop.

We walk down the cobbled streets toward the edge of the ocean. I can smell the sea air, and even though it's getting dark, it's still pretty hot. Springfield is freezing by this time of night.

I see an old castle on the edge of a cliff they call el Morro. I recognize it from the book on the plane. We find a place to sit where a crowd has gathered. María chats with Angela and Hilda.

"She acts tough, but she's the best daughter any father could ask for," Sergio says, beaming.

"She's incredible," my mom replies. "I can't believe how much she's grown. Where does the time go?"

"I don't know," he says. "She's leaving for Florida next year, and I don't know if I can handle being so far away from her. And I really don't like to fly. Maybe I can take a boat?"

I wonder how it feels to have a dad who misses you before you are even gone. Maybe my dad feels that way and I just don't know it.

"I tell her to go to school here and work on the farm with me, but she has her own dreams," he says. "What can I do? They have to fly on their own at some point, ¿no?"

"Yeah," my mom says.

"We're trying to grow the business, but Darma is so focused on the agricultural school," he says. "She's like a mother to me. I have to respect her wishes."

My mom tells me that Darma is Sergio's aunt. Both of Sergio's parents passed away when Sergio was only ten years old, and Darma raised him and his brother.

"She taught me everything I know," he says fondly.

My mom tells him that I wanted to come here to find my dad but that really she just wants some time away with her kids. She talks about working so much and not spending enough time with us. It's strange watching her open up like this. Sergio seems affected by what my mom's saying. He looks over at us a few times and nods.

"Well, we should go look for him," he says.

My mom seems surprised. "Aren't you two in a fight right now?"

"We have different ways of talking to Tía Darma. His way is not very effective. But I can tell finding him is important to Marcus."

I appreciate what Sergio says. I'm not used to asking for help. I can mostly take care of myself and my family.

Fireworks suddenly bursting in the sky make me lose my train of thought. Charlie watches without blinking. He covers his ears whenever there is a loud blast, but for the most part he watches intensely as the lights flicker blue and red and yellow. He points whenever he likes one a lot. He tells me to look, look, look, even though I'm already watching. I lift the camera and disappear behind the lens. *Snap. Snap. Snap.*

I snap a few more pictures, then my mom takes my hand and puts her other arm around Charlie. There we are, our first trip this far away, watching the night turn

121

to sparkles and light, in a place we haven't been, with strangers who say they're family.

❀❀❀

When the fireworks show is over, Sergio suggests we go to a café to have a snack. We all head down to an area close to Tío Ermenio's that has a whole bunch of restaurants. Music blasts from a club with bright neon lights. It's the kind of music Charlie was listening to on his headphones, and he starts grooving in the middle of the street. I try to stop him, but before I can, Angela and Hilda join in and start a dance party. My brother is not a shy kid. Actually, he's a total ham. The more attention he gets from Angela and Hilda, the more he sways to the music.

Sergio starts clapping along, and I see María smile also. Charlie has captured the attention of some people nearby, and soon they start dancing around my brother. A circle forms with Charlie at the center. More gather around, making it harder to keep an eye on Charlie. I manage to see that he's holding Angela's and Hilda's hands as they twist and shake around. Some guy wearing sunglasses, a really tight shirt, and white pants jumps into the middle of the circle. I start moving through the crowd because I don't like the way this guy is surrounding my brother in half-dance steps.

The guy skips and jumps around, keeping his eyes

on Charlie. Angela and Hilda have made room for the guy, who stops right in front of Charlie and stares at him. I feel my hands clench into fists.

Charlie keeps dancing like nothing's wrong as the guy lifts his sunglasses. He's not smiling. He's going to push my brother. I just know it. I rush over to stop him, but I worry I won't get there in time. Before I reach Charlie, he strikes a pose and does an impressive dance twirl. The guy nods, smiles, jumps up, and lands in a split. How in the heck can he do the splits with pants so tight?

Everyone takes a step back and I find myself dead center. Everyone cheers.

No way. No way. They're ridiculous if they think I'm going to dance. Forget it.

I walk back to the edge of the circle, but somebody gently pushes me in again. Charlie takes my hand. I don't move. I allow him to use my hands and arms to twist around, but my feet stay firmly planted on the ground.

I don't dance.

The dance circle expands when my mom joins in. The tight-pants guy starts dancing with my mom, and then Angela and Hilda come back in. I see Sergio trying to urge María to join him in the circle. María says no. She's the only one I relate to in this bizarre situation.

The song ends and people start to disperse. My mom and Sergio find us a table at an outdoor café just steps away. We all make our way over and order some sandwiches. Two other people we don't know join us at our lopsided table. One of them, a lady wearing a hot-pink shirt, shares that she just got her tax return and is treating herself to a night out before she puts the rest into her savings account.

My mom whispers, "I love how friendly people in PR are."

She means Puerto Rico. It's like my mom is some-one else. I don't think I've ever seen her smile so freely. I nod, although I can't understand why the lady is shar-ing so much of her personal information with complete strangers.

The tight-pants dance guy pulls up a chair. He rubs Charlie's head and says that Charlie is a great dancer. He tells us he just broke up with his girlfriend of two years and is now living with his mother in Arecibo but that he stays with his cousin in Old San Juan on the weekends to work as a barista.

Like my mom, I can tell Charlie is really enjoying himself, which makes me feel proud. I wonder if my dad would dance in a situation like this. I think he would probably keep his feet firmly on the ground, like me.

When the night is finally over, we all head back to Tío Ermenio's.

"We should travel more," my mom says. "This one night has been incredible."

"Let's check Dad's room, Mom," I tell her. "We might find something."

"Hmm?"

We open the door to the hostel and Tío Ermenio pops his head up from the sofa in the living room.

"How was your night, muchachos?" he asks, getting up and tightening the belt of his bathrobe.

Before anyone can answer, I say, "I wonder if we could check in my dad's old room."

"Honey, it's late," my mom says. "We can do that tomorrow."

"It's just upstairs, Mom," I reply. "It's on the way."

Tío Ermenio takes out a key and hands it to me. "The boy will sleep better if his mind is at ease," he says to my mom.

She sighs. I head upstairs and am surprised when the rest of the group follows me. I guess they're curious to see what's in there too.

I slowly turn the key to my dad's old room, and we all pour in. I find a light switch, and the first thing I spot is a whole bunch of books on a desk. There's one about farm machines. There's another one about starting your own business and another about fruits and vegetables.

"He had plans," Sergio offers. "Big ones. Too big, perhaps."

What's wrong with big plans? I skim through one of

the books. It's mostly in Spanish, but I can tell from the pictures and the title that it has something to do with agricultural tourism in Puerto Rico.

I put the book down and scan the room. There are a few shirts on a rack. A blue suitcase with wheels is parked next to the bed, and there are a few papers on the night table.

"I left everything as he did," Tío Ermenio says, walking around back to the doorway. "I wanted to keep his room ready for when he returned. Even though we had a disagreement, family is family."

With that, Tío Ermenio quietly leaves the room.

"Has anyone tried calling him?" I ask Sergio.

"He doesn't have a phone," he replies.

"Who tries to start a business without having a phone?" my mom blurts out. "Marcus, honey, can we go now? It's late."

Mom has a point. Why doesn't my dad have a phone? And what happened with Tío Ermenio that made him storm off? The way Sergio talks about my dad, it doesn't seem like he likes him very much. I notice that his voice sounds slightly irritated when the subject comes up. My mom's eye rolls make it clear how she feels. It's like they're ganging up on my dad. It doesn't seem fair.

"Mira esto," María says, holding a piece of paper in her hand. Charlie looks at it and starts to read.

"Orocovis, Marcus. Here. Look." Charlie hands me the paper.

"Yeah, I think that has to do with a restaurant your dad wanted to open in Darma's town. Another one of your father's plans," Sergio says. "Listen, we are going back to the farm tomorrow morning. Would you like to see it? You are all welcome!"

"You don't need to stay for the farmers' market?" Mom asks.

"We typically come into town on the weekends. We stayed an extra day to pick up Angela and Hilda at the airport. They wanted to stay an extra night to see Old San Juan and, well, you know how it goes."

"How does what go?" I ask him, confused.

"My daughter and her friends wanted to stay an extra night, so we did." Sergio looks at me. "We have to go back to Orocovis tomorrow to pick up produce for the market this coming weekend. You can come with us if you like."

"Yes," I say, without a second thought. If my dad was opening a restaurant near Darma's farm, maybe he's there, running his business.

"No," my mom says, taking the letter. This isn't her relaxed voice anymore. She's serious. "This is not what I wanted to do on my vacation, Marcus. If your father returns my email, we'll go see him. But I'm not dragging Sergio and María on some wild goose chase to look for someone who doesn't want to be found. . . ."

"It would be no problem for us, Mel," Sergio says. "Honestly. And Tía Darma would love to see you."

My mom looks at me, then back at Sergio.

"There's plenty of room in our truck," he continues. "And the boys will love Orocovis. It will be, as you say, an adventure."

"Can we stop by the chinchorros?" Hilda chimes in. "They are so much fun!"

"Hilda," Angela jumps in. "It's rude to impose."

"What?" Hilda responds. "They will love the chinchorros!"

Angela shakes her head. "Always thinking of the next good time," she mutters, then says something that sounds like "father" in German.

Hilda explains that chinchorros are the best places to soak in island life. They are little roadside shacks that serve snacks and refreshing drinks. It's where locals catch up with each other. María agrees that it's something we should experience, since it's our first trip to Puerto Rico.

Sergio tells us more about the farm. He makes it sound like it's the greatest place in the world.

The excitement builds. Eventually, even Mom can't turn down the offer.

"Okay, we'll see everyone out front after breakfast," Sergio says. "You're going to love the countryside," Sergio says to Charlie.

Charlie leans on me and puts his arm around my waist. This wasn't part of the plan, and I can tell that he's feeling a little nervous.

"Don't worry, man. I'll be there," I say.

María smiles at Charlie. Then he turns to me and says, "I'm not nervous!" He pushes past me and starts walking upstairs. What's that about?

We say good night to Tío Ermenio and walk up the many flights of stairs to our rooftop shack in the middle of Old San Juan. We cross the bridge, which is now lit by white Christmas lights strung up throughout the courtyard. My mom decides she wants to shower again. I'm telling you, she's in love with it. Charlie changes into his pajamas, plops down on the netted bed, and falls asleep immediately.

I change and climb onto the twin bed in the corner. My legs dangle off the end, but it doesn't bother me. My mom's humming in the shower mixes with the music still blasting from the streets below.

I close my eyes and let sleep wash over me. Tomorrow Mom, Charlie, María, Angela, Hilda, Sergio, and I will take a drive into the country to go to a farm and ask about my dad.

Finally, a lead.

DAY TWO

THIRTEEN
FINCA VEGA

I wake up to the smell of coffee and freshly baked pastries. When I sit up and stretch in bed, I notice I'm alone in the room. My mom and Charlie must already be at breakfast. After I get ready and leave the shack, I spot Tío Ermenio on the rooftop, setting out more pastries. My mom is already out there, chatting with him and Sergio. She waves when she sees me.

"Hey, sleepyhead!"

My mom tells me it's ten o'clock in the morning. I can't remember the last time I slept that late. Charlie has already had three guava pastries and wants another, but my mom says no. She offers one to me and I take a bite. It's not bad.

"And try Ermenio's café con leche!"

I take a sip of the sweet milky coffee and my head gets cloudy. I don't like sweet things. After breakfast, my mom heads back to the room to pack a small bag for us. Just in case, she says. Then we head downstairs to meet the rest of the crew. Angela and Hilda are dressed like we're going on a hike. María is wearing a dress that my mom totally loves.

"What a lovely pattern for a summer dress, María. You look beautiful."

"Thank you," she replies.

"Okay, everyone!" Sergio calls out. "The truck is running and ready for our road trip adventure!"

We all walk outside and pause at the edge of the sidewalk.

"What is that?" Charlie blurts out.

"That is our ride," María huffs. She looks at her dad and shakes her head disapprovingly. "My dad refuses to trade in this cacharro trying to pass for a truck."

"What are you talking about? You love this truck! It has character!"

The pickup has a covering on the bed that I guess they use to transport the vegetables and fruits. There is a backseat, but it doesn't look very comfortable. And the truck is lime green and has a hand-painted circle with FRUTAS Y VEGGIES—FINCA VEGA written in the middle.

"It has the character of a three-legged donkey," María says. "Interesting to look at but not advisable to ride on."

"Angela, do you remember the bus in Senegal?" Hilda says, laughing.

Angela nods. "I can't believe it didn't tip over."

"There were maybe thirty people on that little bus! So much fun!"

"And dangerous," Angela says.

My mom asks what they were doing in Senegal, and they say that their dad works for a humanitarian aid company and they were helping out during the summer.

"The whole family goes," Angela says.

Angela and Hilda talk about their parents a lot. It seems like they do a lot of stuff together.

Sergio continues to make his case for the lime-green, two-door, small-backseat pickup truck we're all staring at. Hilda and Angela look at each other and shrug.

"We've done it before."

They open the door of the pickup truck and dive into the backseat. My mom and Charlie look at me, and I just shake my head.

"Come! We fit! We fit!" Hilda says, patting the seat, indicating there is more room. María sighs.

"Papi, this isn't going to work," she says.

"The backseat fits four people!" Sergio says.

"¿Y Marcus? Who is taller than all of us?"

Sergio realizes that there is no way I can fit in the backseat.

"He'll go in the front!"

María sighs and squeezes next to Hilda. Angela sits directly behind the front passenger seat.

My mom manages a smile. "Adventure?"

"In a lime-green pickup truck," I say.

Charlie doesn't seem fazed, which surprises me. He goes around to the other side of the car and hops in next to María. He smiles at her lovingly. She smiles back and pats his hand.

"Tight squeeze, ¿eh, lindo?"

"Yes," Charlie says. It's clear that he likes the way María calls him beautiful.

My mom squeezes in next to him. They fit like a bunch of circus clowns packed into a Beetle. Sergio goes around to the driver's side and hops in. I push the passenger seat into place. There isn't much space for me, but it is way more than anybody has in the back. I try to move the seat forward a little to give them room, but the seat continues to slide without clicking into place.

"The seat doesn't lock anymore," Sergio says. "You have to hang on to the handle up there so it doesn't slide back and forth too much."

He's got to be kidding, right? Sergio moves a stick

jutting out of the middle and revs the engine. The truck lurches forward and back a few times before plowing ahead. My seat slides every time the car moves. I dig my feet into the corner of the floor and grab the armrest in order to keep stable. Tío Ermenio says he's staying behind in case anybody comes by needing a place to stay. He waves good-bye as we bounce and rock down the cobblestone street. His face looks a bit sad, like maybe he wishes he could be crammed into this car too. I really hope he doesn't ask. I like Tío Ermenio, but it would be impossible to fit another person into this truck. I'd end up in the back with the empty vegetable crates.

Sergio offers a smile with each major bump we go over. "She just needs some time to get used to all of us."

We chug along the roads, and before long we're on the highway heading toward the countryside. Sergio says the drive to Tía Darma's farm is about an hour and thirty-five minutes.

"Darma's farm is just outside Orocovis," María offers.

"Then we can check out the place in Orocovis your dad wanted to open," Sergio says.

My dad's books on agriculture and opening a business made it seem like he maybe wanted to open a restaurant. Why does Sergio seem so annoyed by that?

I look at the paper from my dad's room that I saved in my pocket. It's a letter that says something about a small restaurant for sale in Orocovis. I think he started off as a farmer and then wanted to open a restaurant. Makes sense to me.

"Tía Darma will have an idea where he might be. She knows everything about her town."

This trip to the farm might give me some answers. I take pictures as we drive because I want to document every step. *Snap.* The twisting roads along the highway. *Snap.* The old homes. *Snap.* The far-off mountain ranges. *Snap. Snap. Snap.* The jam-packed car. *Snap. Snap.* My brother staring out the window. *Snap.* My mother's gaze, lost in the clouds. *Snap.*

Angela bounces and accidentally pushes my seat forward. "Oh, sorry, Marcus."

"That's okay," I say.

Sergio drives and moves the little stick in between us every time he wants to go faster. I keep locking my legs so the seat doesn't shift, but I'm afraid I'm going to break through the bottom of the truck.

"And we'll get back to Tío Ermenio's today?" my mom asks. I'm wondering the same.

"We should be fine, unless it rains. This truck doesn't do well in the rain. But I didn't see rain in the forecast."

I'm glad my mom brought a day bag after all, "just

in case." We drive through the highway for a while and then off-road toward Orocovis.

"The heart of Puerto Rico," Sergio says. "Literally. It's right in the middle."

After about an hour, we're completely surrounded by green mountains. A thick mist wraps us up. We've swapped bright and sunny Old San Juan, where you can hear and smell the ocean from the streets, for these winding mountain roads. It feels like a completely different planet out here.

"There are many places to visit," Sergio continues as our unofficial tour guide. "Many famous musicians were born here, which is why they call this region the center of music in Puerto Rico. But really, it's the history of the Taíno and their work on the agriculture of the region that's really impressive."

Sergio tells us that the Taíno were the indigenous population on the island.

"Taíno heritage runs deep in Puerto Rico," Sergio says. "Even to this day."

I look in the rearview mirror and see that Charlie is peacefully sleeping on María. The truck hums and bumps along as we all quietly take in the scenery. We turn down another road and head into an area dense with trees. Past the trees, the road gets bumpier. The truck slows as we approach a wooden gate. There's a sign on it that looks like it's a hundred years old.

FINCA VEGA

PIEDRA SIN AGUA NO AGUZA EN LA FRAGUA

"What does it mean?" I ask.

"It translates to 'Vega Farm.'"

"What about the quote on the bottom?"

"It literally means," María says, answering for her dad, "'Stone without water doesn't sharpen in the forge.'"

"I don't get it," I say.

"Nobody does," María says.

Sergio tries to explain. "That is the literal meaning, yes, but what's really being said is, 'From nothing, nothing can come.'"

I still don't get it, but I don't say anything. María shakes her head and tells me not to worry about it. Some things can't be translated, I guess.

Sergio gets out and starts to open the gate. He's struggling, so I go help. The air is thick, and the rustle of the trees makes me feel like I'm way smaller than I really am. I walk over to Sergio and my shoes squish into the ground.

"Careful," he says. "The horses come through here also."

Great. I stepped in horse poop. After a closer look, I realize it's just a muddy hole. I help Sergio pull open the gate and he rushes back to the car.

"I've got to get a moving start," he says. "I can't stop or the truck will stall. Can you shut the gate after I drive across?"

I nod.

"I just have to get up that little hill over there and then we'll wait for you at the top. It's not that far to walk, but this truck isn't the most reliable thing in the world, you know?"

Sergio, the understater of the century.

He revs up the lime-green truck and zips through. One wheel catches in a mud hole and starts spinning. The spinning almost takes me out. Sergio regains control and zips up the incline that starts just inside the gate. The truck chugs to the top, and all I can see is the taillight glowing on the hill. I close the gate and put the little rope back around the post and make my way up the hill slowly, careful to avoid more mud holes or worse, horse poop. When I get to the top, Hilda is posing for Angela, who is taking pictures with the miles and miles of rolling green hills as the backdrop.

"Papa wants so many pictures," Hilda says.

"And my sister is in all of them," Angela adds.

"I'll take one of you too," Hilda says. "After a few more of me."

"I can take one of both of you," I offer. Hilda takes her sister's hand and poses before I even take my camera out. She makes funny faces while her sister tries to get into place. They're so different, but they seem really close. Angela never seems too upset with her sister. Only mildly annoyed. I get like that with Charlie sometimes. But never for too long.

My mom gets out to stretch her legs. Charlie refuses to. When he fell asleep, we were still in San Juan. Now we're somewhere else.

"You all right, man?" I ask him through the window. He ignores me. He's not happy.

"It's really beautiful out here, huh, sweetie?" My mom puts her arm on my shoulder.

I nod.

We finish our pit stop and hop back in the car, making our way down to the farm. The tiny road makes us feel like we are the only people on the entire planet in this lime-green sardine can in the middle of a misty green forest.

After a few minutes of driving, we come to a house with a main entrance and two smaller entrances on each side. It isn't big compared to some houses in Springfield, but it's certainly bigger than our little brown house back home.

We get closer and it's clear that one of the smaller entrances is actually a stable. An old guy leads a horse out of it.

Sergio finds a parking spot close to the main house

and we all tumble out. Everyone except Charlie. He still doesn't want to get out of the car.

"Come on, sweetie," my mom urges.

I tell him about the horse in the stable. That gets his attention.

"Seriously, man," I say. "It was over there. I can show you if you want."

He watches me carefully. "Where?" he says, getting out.

"Over there," I say. "Follow me."

"I wanna see too!" my mom says.

As we get closer to the stable, the smell gets stronger.

"What is that?" Charlie asks, holding his nose.

"What do you think, man?"

We get to the stables and peek inside. Hooves clopping and heavy huffing fills the room. The smell is a combination of hay and sweaty animal. I don't care how beautiful you think horses are. They stink.

Charlie holds his nose but walks deeper into the stable. A dark brown horse with a white spot on its muzzle trots to the edge of its gate and stops. It notices us. It moves its hooves slightly back and forth. It bows and huffs.

"Careful, man," I tell Charlie, who keeps getting closer and closer to the horse. "That beast looks like it doesn't like that we're in here."

Charlie keeps moving in and the horse edges closer

to its gate. Charlie smiles and the horse exhales heavily. If that gate opens, the horse could bolt out and crush us. Charlie is right in the line of fire.

"You're too close, man. Back up."

Charlie extends his hand. The horse continues to shuffle back and forth, nodding.

"I don't think he likes all the attention, man. Don't put your hand out."

"Honey," my mom adds, "listen to your brother."

But he doesn't. He keeps his hand out. I walk toward him because I don't know what that horse is going to do. I get to him, but before I pull his arm away, the horse gently nudges my brother's hand with the top of its muzzle. Charlie's smile grows wider. He rubs the horse affectionately.

"Magia no le gusta a nadie."

I turn around to find an old woman standing behind us. She's wearing jeans, construction boots, a purple tank top, and a wide-brimmed hat. Her face is solemn as she walks toward my brother and the horse.

"Hola, chico," she says to Charlie. Her voice is deep and raspy, like she just woke up from a long nap. "You like the horse?" she asks.

Charlie nods.

"Her name is Magic," the old lady says. "She doesn't like many people. She only responds when someone is nítido."

"What does that mean?" I ask.

"Someone who is sharp," she says. "Someone she can see clearly. I am Darma. Welcome to Finca Vega."

She turns back to Magic, rubs her mane, and then puts her arm around Charlie.

"Come with me," she says. "Lunch is already prepared. I made fresh limonada and a delicious flan de coco for dessert."

My mom and I stare at each other as Charlie and Darma walk out of the stable and toward the farmhouse. Charlie walks with her like he's known her all his life.

FOURTEEN
GETTING GOOD DARMA

"I'm glad I picked up the phone when Sergio called," Darma says, bringing us into the house, where the rest of our crew has already started eating sandwiches. "It's so nice to see you and your boys, Melissa. But I don't like that I've never met them in person until now."

Mom sags a little. "I know," she says. "It's hard to see time pass when you're just trying to make each day happen."

Darma's face is stern but not angry. "Weeds need to be uprooted if the seeds are to grow."

Darma is intimidating like Yoda is intimidating. She's small and wrinkled but with a face that says, *I'm packing a lightsaber in my construction boot.*

She pats my mom on the shoulder and sits down at the head of the table.

There's a pitcher of something that looks exactly like lemonade. Charlie grabs a sandwich and sits next to Darma. He immediately starts asking her questions. Darma seems to lean in a little to try to understand exactly what he says.

I take a seat next to them and chime in. "He wants to know how many horses you have."

Like I said, people who just meet my brother don't always understand him.

"Yes, I know," she responds. "I asked him if he'd ever ridden one."

Darma continues to talk to Charlie, and my mom and I turn to each other.

"Well, he's connected with Tía Darma pretty well," Mom says.

My brother pretty much ignores me throughout lunch. The more comfortable he gets with Darma, the more he talks to her. He even helps her clear the table when we finish lunch.

My brother has a lot of abilities. Wanting to clean is not one of them. Whenever we have dinner together at home, Charlie always pretends he's too tired to help clean. Sometimes he'll put his head down on the table and pretend to be asleep until I've cleared our plates. What the heck has Tía Darma done to him?

Just a few days ago, I thought my family consisted of Charlie and my mom. And my dad, I guess. Now we've got all these cousins and great-aunts and uncles all over Puerto Rico. It's strange.

"We haven't all sat down for a meal like this in a while," my mom says.

I nod.

"It's not always going to be you and Charlie eating alone, sweetie. As soon as I can get that promotion . . ."

"I know, Mom," I tell her, because I don't want her to beat herself up about it. "You know, Dad—"

"What about him?" she says before I can finish my thought.

"I just . . ." I start. "I just think it might be different now, you know? He might be really excited to see us. And we've got this whole family down here."

My mom's silence makes me uncomfortable. She might not think my father has changed, but I do. The memories I have of him aren't all bad. Yes, I remember the way my mom's eyes were puffy for a long time after he left. But I also remember when my dad took me to the zoo. I think I was three and he had me on his shoulders. It was bright and hot so he gave me his baseball hat. The hat was way too big and it made me sweaty, but I didn't take it off. My mom was there. She had a round belly. I don't remember what he said to me, but I remember him holding my legs. I remember feeling safe.

"Hon?" My mom snaps me out of this memory. "You okay?"

I nod.

"Come on. Let's go help out in the kitchen."

Everyone is already there, helping to dry and put dishes away, wash pots and pans. There are a few people who aren't part of our group, wearing aprons. Maybe they work here?

A large guy walks in from the back door and into the kitchen. The smell of stable and hay follows him in. He takes off his hat and puts it to his chest. He speaks in mumbled Spanish and I can't understand him at all, but his tone sounds worried. Darma nods and excuses herself from the kitchen.

She starts out the door with the big guy, and Charlie follows.

"We'll talk more later, okay? Right now I have to tend to a sick cow," she says, stroking Charlie's hair.

"Tía," Sergio says before Darma gets outside. "La medicina. You can give her the medicine I got from the vet. He says it might help."

Tía Darma watches Sergio carefully. "Take the boys on a tour of the house," she says, like she's not interested in hearing Sergio's suggestion.

"I wanna go with you," Charlie says. "I wanna see the sick cow."

Darma looks at my mom. "I have a better idea," Tía

Darma says. "Go explore the house and when I return, I'll introduce you to Paco."

"Who's that?" Charlie asks. You can tell that he has serious doubts that Paco is more interesting than a sick cow.

"Paco is our prized toro. He's the biggest bull in all of Orocovis."

"A bull?"

"Yes," she says, "a very big one. Only the bravest dare come close. And I know for a fact you are one of the bravest."

Charlie likes this. He puffs up his chest.

Darma leaves with the big guy, and the rest of us finish cleaning the kitchen. Charlie is suddenly not interested in cleaning anymore.

"What happened? Lost the will to clean?" I tell him, teasing him with a rag.

"Meh," he says, sitting on a barstool in the middle of the kitchen.

"Cheer up, Charlie," Sergio says. "Let me show you the courtyard garden."

We follow him out. Sergio walks with me and explains that Aunt Darma loves gardening.

"She's focusing more on teaching agriculture than raising livestock these days," he says. "There are so many unique fruits and vegetables in Puerto Rico. See this here?" Sergio points to an orange-and-yellow flower with spikes. "This is called rambutan." He holds it carefully. "It is a fruit similar in taste to lychee."

"An alien!" Charlie shouts.

"It does look like an alien, Charlie," Sergio says, laughing. "The name means 'hairy fruit.' But inside, it is delicious and very high in nutrients."

Sergio carefully pulls a rambutan off its stem and gently cuts into it with his pocketknife. He splits the hairy exterior and out pops a slimy white ball.

"Here, take a bite. Just be careful with the seed in the middle."

Charlie and I both stare as Sergio offers it to us.

"Oh, come on, guys!" My mom takes the fruit and expertly chews and spits out the seed. "It's delicious."

Charlie looks at Mom as if he's afraid she's about to turn into an extraterrestrial. I'm probably making the same face.

"It originally comes from Malaysia but grows very well in Puerto Rico. She likes our weather." Sergio winks as he pulls off another rambutan. He offers it to me. I take it and feel its leathery spikes. Sergio holds out his pocketknife.

"Maybe I'll try it later," I tell him, returning the fruit.

"Hold on to it," he says.

I put the fruit in my cargo shorts. Charlie completely refuses to take one.

"No way, man," he says. "No way."

I look up from the middle of the courtyard. There isn't a ceiling, just four columns surrounding the wooden square where several strange plants and vegetables are growing. I recognize small tomatoes and a lot of green leaves everywhere.

"Oh my goodness, is that spinach?" my mom asks, bending over to get a closer look.

"When I was little, my parents used to leave me with Tía Darma for the summer," Sergio says. "They traveled a lot. We made this garden when I turned nine. Instead of giving me a toy truck or clothes, Darma brought out some dirt and wood and said my birthday present was going to be a garden. I wasn't happy about that."

"But look at it now!" my mom says, smelling more leaves. "She gave you a gift that can last forever if you care for it."

"That's what she told me. I still wanted a monster truck, though."

My mom shakes her head.

"What? I was nine! Who wants a garden when they're nine?"

"I would," my mom says. "I always wanted a garden. I thought I was going to live in a place where I could garden year-round." My mom's expression goes from dreamy to droopy again.

"Mom?" I ask.

"Yeah, sweetie?"

"Maybe Dad came back to Puerto Rico because he wanted to build a farm of his own? Didn't Tío Ermenio say he loved coming to Orocovis?"

"Farms aren't built, Marcus," my mom says, moving through the columns. "They grow after being cared for."

There's a wooden sign staked in the corner. It looks like it's written by someone just learning to spell.

SERGIO'S GARTEN

"She left it misspelled that way so I would never forget how to spell 'garden' again," Sergio says. "Come, there are gardens all over the house."

We snake around corridor after corridor. Angela and Hilda stop at every little garden. There are beds of squash, root vegetables Sergio calls yucca, and a tree with big green fruit that looks like spiky footballs.

"Those are called guanabana," Sergio explains.

There are bright red furry things called achiote. The theme is weird-looking fruit no one has ever heard of, I guess. Nobody in my school would go near these. Except maybe Danny. He probably would. That reminds me. I take out his camera. *Snap. Snap. Snap.* I don't know if it's possible for a camera to capture every color on these fruits. There are signs everywhere with squiggly names scrawled on them. They look like they were all written by young kids. Sergio says Darma never had children, but she had lots of nephews and nieces and students from her school. She made them all plant gardens.

I look up at another ceiling-less roof. The sky has turned grayer than when we arrived. From above, Darma's house must look like it has a hundred holes punched into it. We go through a set of doors and enter a living room.

"This is the proper house," María says, walking with Charlie. He has seemed to warm up to this new place. It's like he knows it. Is this what my dad felt like when he was my age walking through this house?

Inside Darma's living room there are pictures hanging everywhere. Maybe thousands.

"This is the family," Sergio says.

I scan around, but I don't see my dad in any of the pictures.

Sergio notices.

"Your dad . . ." he starts. "When we were kids, we had this dream to buy a farm together. Finca Primo Vega. The Vega Cousins' Farm. When we got older, the plan was to save enough money to buy the land and build the farm. Tía Darma said your father was too untethered and impatient. When he came back one day after years of being gone, she told him what she thought of his choices. Your dad got upset and left the farm life behind forever. I couldn't convince him to make amends.

He said he had other plans. Tía was right, I guess. Your father never settles."

I turn back to the photos. What's wrong with not settling? Isn't that what they teach people? To never settle.

I step outside to get some fresh air and Mom follows me.

The green mountains here feel like they're breathing, like the mist all around us is the air they exhale to the clouds above. It feels like we're at the highest point in the world. I aim the camera.

Suddenly, a shot cracks the air and echoes across the mountains. The rest of the crew rushes outside to where Mom and I are standing.

Was that a gun? Charlie runs to me and digs his head into my side. I put my arm around him. Along the side of the house, Darma walks slowly toward us. She hands a large pistol to the big guy from earlier and tells him something out of earshot. She reaches my mom and me first.

"It's going to rain," she says matter-of-factly, like a gunshot didn't just blast throughout the entire mountain range.

Charlie, hearing Darma, lifts his head.

"Darma!" he says excitedly. He starts detailing what happened as best he can.

He points to the hills and tells Darma that a "big boom came from over there!"

"Yes," she says. "I said good-bye to a sick cow."

If that's how she says good-bye, no wonder my dad wanted his own farm.

Sergio shakes his head, and I hear him mutter something about the cow just needing medicine. Darma pats Charlie on the back. She looks at me, then at Sergio.

"Sometimes the necessary thing isn't always the easiest," she says, heading inside. "The roads will be too dangerous for you," she continues. "No driving back to Viejo San Juan tonight."

I look at my mom.

"I'm not arguing with her," she says.

Darma stops at the door and waits for everyone to file inside. When I reach the door, she stops me. She's way shorter than I am, but I suddenly feel very small next to this lady who just shot a cow and doesn't seem affected by it.

"I have seen your father," she says, watching me carefully. "But tonight we will not discuss it. Understand?"

I nod. What else am I going to do?

Darma says Charlie and I will bunk with Sergio. My mom will have her own room. Angela, Hilda, and María will share a room. My mom asks Sergio about cell service.

"Marcus, give me my phone, honey," she says. "I want to call Tío Ermenio."

My mom follows Sergio outside with the phone. I go too. Out there, the evening air fills with strange sounds coming from the darkness.

"The coquí," Sergio says. "That little frog has made its way into our art, poetry, and music for centuries."

"That's a frog?" I ask, listening.

"Yes, it's saying, 'co-kee, co-kee.'" Sergio imitates the strange frog's sound. "That's where it gets its name."

"Isn't it beautiful?" Mom asks. "It's like they're singing to us."

It's a little creepy listening to the singing frogs as it gets darker, but I don't say anything.

Sergio takes us to a little area near the barn where my mom has to stand on a haystack to get reception.

"When the hay is used to feed the cows and horses, there is no cell service," Sergio jokes.

My mom finds a signal and calls Tío Ermenio. She tells him we're staying the night and that we'll call him first thing in the morning. I guess she doesn't want him to worry. Mom hangs up, hands me the phone, and hops down from the haystack.

She smiles awkwardly. "Adventure?"

A sleepover at our cow-murdering great-aunt's farm in the middle of nowhere with little singing frogs "co-keeing" everywhere. What's not adventurous about that?

We go back inside, where Darma is already plating

our dinner. It's a dish called asopao. It's like a tomato rice soup with chicken and lots of vegetables. Actually, that's exactly what it is.

Charlie doesn't seem to mind being here. Darma continues chatting with him while she sips from a gigantic coffee mug.

Finally, she tells us all that it's time for bed. She doesn't give us an option.

"The rain will come," she says. "It will be dangerous along the hills, so no going outside."

Nobody argues.

Later that night I sneak out and head to the haystack. I climb up, careful not to fall over. I point the phone to the sky and check for a signal. I see lightning illuminate the dark mountains like the flashbulb on my camera. Seconds later, thunder echoes across the range. I check my email. Still no response. I type a quick note.

Hey,

We're in Orocovis, at Tia Darma's farm.

**She killed a cow. She said it was sick.
Have you ever done that?**

**Okay, gotta go. There's lightning and I
don't want to get fried by a bolt. I'm on**

that haystack. Have you ever used it to
make a call when you were here? Oh, wait.
You don't have a phone. I hope you get
this.

Bye,
Marcus

I go back inside and get into bed. Soon the rain
starts to pound the ceiling. I think of my dad. Did he
challenge Darma? Did he disagree with her? What did
he do to get kicked out of this farm in the clouds?

DAY THREE

FIFTEEN

ECHOES OF THE MOUNTAINS

The next morning, Charlie and I wake up at about the same time and find Mom in the living room.

"I woke up early and had coffee with Darma," she says, stretching. She takes a sip of coffee. "What an incredible woman. Did you know that her family has owned this farm for over a hundred years? She's lived on the farm her entire life. She didn't have internet until two years ago, when Sergio insisted she needed to modernize. She has a flip phone, but she hates to use it."

My mom says Darma is an inspiration.

"She buses kids from all over the island and teaches them about farming," she says.

"Does she teach them how to kill cows?" I ask.

Charlie takes a pretend shot at the ground and makes a horrible mooing sound.

"Yeah, Darma is a great influence," I tell her sarcastically.

Mom ignores me and says, "I could easily move here."

Say what?

She goes on and on about how inspired she feels here.

"How amazing would it be?"

"Did she find any information about Dad?" I ask, changing the subject.

My mom reacts like I just snapped her out of a dream.

At that exact moment, Darma walks in. She always has creepy timing. "He asked me for money," she says. "And he ignored his basic, most fundamental duty."

"What is that?" I ask.

Darma takes Charlie by the hand. He offers her a hug and she brings him in. She kisses him on the forehead and rubs the back of his neck while she looks at me. She starts to say something, then stops herself. She takes a sip of coffee.

"He wasn't ready to own a farm," she continues. "He did not respect my decision. Then he left."

Why wouldn't she help out her own family?

"Where is he now?" I finally ask.

"Your father," Darma says, her tone lighter than before, "is too impatient. He wants things to come quickly and easily. You cannot farm that way. He thinks money will solve all problems. It will not."

"But where is he?" I say, getting slightly irritated. My mom shoots me a look that tells me I should watch my attitude.

"He wanders," she says. "One day he is driving a food truck; the next day he is working at a hotel. I called my cousin Pepe in Manatí. He says, up until a few months ago, your father would stay there from time to time. I think they're still in touch."

Even though it sounds like my dad has a lot of tíos and tías to turn to, I wonder if he's lonely. Does he like wandering?

I look at my mom.

"Marcus," she says, sounding annoyed. "At some point you're going to have to let go of this."

Why should I let it go? He's my dad.

Darma puts her hand on my mom's shoulder and together they go outside. Charlie follows. I slowly make my way outside also. Mom and Darma watch the landscape quietly. Darma stands while my mom sits in a rocking chair, quietly looking out. What is so bad about wanting things to come quickly? About never settling? Why don't they just give him a chance? People assume that because I'm big, I'm going to cause harm. They don't give me a chance. It's all unfair.

After everyone finishes breakfast, we say good-bye to Darma. She packs us some lunch and a few gallons of water for the road. Sergio loads two boxes of plantains into the back of the pickup. He has to deliver them to a neighbor about twenty miles away.

My mom hugs Darma and thanks her.

"The seeds will continue to grow, Melissa. When you return, you will see how they've blossomed."

Darma takes my mom's face in her hands. I notice a few tears run down my mom's face.

Mom wants to be a farmer now? How is that going to solve our problems? The whole reason we're in Puerto Rico in the first place is to find my dad so we can fix our lives in Springfield. He can help us. And spend some time with us. Maybe.

I kick rocks on the way to the car, but before I get in, Darma stops me.

"Be careful with the things you seek," she says.

I don't know what this lady is trying to say to me.

"Thanks for letting us stay," I say, stepping inside Sergio's lime-green truck.

Everyone packs in. Hilda rests her head on Angela's shoulder. They both seem really sleepy. María scoots toward the middle of the backseat.

"You're coming?" Sergio asks his daughter.

"Sí, Papá."

Sergio beams. "She called me Papá," he says. "She hasn't called me that since she was little."

"Stop staring!" María puts her hands over her face, and Sergio quickly takes his eyes off the rearview mirror.

He starts the truck. "Nos vemos mañana, Tía," he calls out to Darma.

"You're going back tomorrow?" my mom asks.

Don't tell me she wants to come back to this farm. We've already wasted a whole day, and we're leaving in three days. We still have no idea where my dad is. We should go to that uncle's house. What was his name? Tío Pepe who lives in Manatí. Or at least go back to Tío Ermenio's to look for more clues. I don't understand why my mom isn't trying harder. I just don't. She knows we're struggling! I stay quiet, though. It isn't anybody's business how I feel.

Charlie snuggles up to Hilda while chomping on a piece of purple fruit that looks like an alien egg.

"Dragon fruit," he says, shoving it into my face.

"Man, get that away from me."

"You feeling okay?" my mom asks.

I ignore her.

"He's grumpy," Charlie says, and grabs one of my ears with his free hand.

I shove him away. "I said stop."

My brother sits back. "Yep, Marcus is grumpy," he whispers loudly.

Darma steps close to the window and leans in.

"Some of the locals say your father still visits the chinchorros on the road to Manatí," she says, watching me carefully.

"That's on our delivery route," Sergio says. "We can drop these things off, then stop by a few of them if you like."

"You don't have to do that," my mom replies. "We're not here for—"

"Chinchorros! Ja!" Hilda says, rubbing Sergio's shoulders.

"She loves those," Angela says. "Although I'm not positive we should be going."

Hilda starts saying something in German that sounds like she's arguing with her sister again. I don't think they're playing around this time. They keep going on like this until María says something that calms both of them.

"Okay?" she says. Hilda doesn't say anything and Angela nods.

"Are they okay?" Mom asks.

"Angela wants to return to Tío Ermenio's. She has to study for a big exam coming up when she goes home next week. Hilda doesn't want to go back."

I want to keep moving. We're wasting time standing here.

"It isn't too out of the way," Sergio says.

"I—I really don't want this to be about searching . . ."

Okay. I've had enough.

"Mom, why don't you want to find him?" I finally say. "Why don't you care?"

She's silent for a moment.

"Marcus," she says, leaning forward to face me in the front seat. "This trip isn't about the search for your father. It's about us, this family—you, me, your brother—getting a break."

"I just don't see—"

"Marcus, you beat up a kid! You hurt him. We need— *I* need a break. Our family is falling apart. I don't know what we're going to do with Charlie, or with you if you get expelled, or if I'm going to get a promotion. I just don't know. I wanted to be here so we can just regroup for a minute. Get away from everything. Be together. Just us."

"What about all these people?" I say, pointing around the tiny car. "Were they part of your 'regroup'?"

"We all have golden tickets, Marcus!" Charlie says.

Charlie must not get how angry I am. And that makes me angrier.

"You leave us at home most of the time, Mom. You come home late; you never have money." Nobody in the car moves or says anything. "And now you come to Puerto Rico and you just want to 'regroup'? Seriously? How do you expect us to regroup if when we go back everything will be the same? Charlie will still have Down syndrome. I will still be a bully to anyone who looks at me. And you, you'll still be gone."

My face stings, and the blood in my fists reaches a boiling point. I slam the dashboard and the truck shakes. The silence is broken when I push myself out of the car, past Darma, and stomp down the hill through the mud toward the farm gate.

"You may not care to find my dad," I say, turning around one last time. "But I do. I care."

The humidity is thick, and sweat forms on my neck. Streams of tears cool my cheeks, but my face still burns. I don't look back. I march forward. Through the mud, down the hill, away from this farm, away from my mom, away from everything and everyone.

I open the gate.

FINCA VEGA

If I'm being honest, I'm mad at my dad, too. Sure, maybe he needed time to figure things out. But ten years? That's a really long time. Didn't he ever wonder how we were doing? How could someone just turn their back on their family and leave? He doesn't even answer my emails. He has to have seen at least one by now. At least one.

I look around. The mist in the mountains covers the trees. Birds caw in the distance. My head spins. My heart beats fast. Too fast. The camera around my neck feels like a cinder block as I turn in every direction. There is nothing but mountains and mist and bird sounds echoing. My head pounds. Finally, I yell.

"Ahhhhhhhhhhhhhhhhhhhhhhhhhhhhhhhhhhhhhh!!!"

My voice thunders across the landscape. The birds flap their wings, probably to go somewhere quieter.

"Ahhhhhhhhhhhhhhhhhhhhhhhhhhhhhhhhhhhhhh!!!"

Now the only sound is my voice carrying across the entire earth. I am bigger than the mountains. I am bigger than the sky. I am the Mastodon of Montgomery Middle, the Springfield Skyscraper, the Moving Mountain, the Terrible Tower. Freakazoid. I am Big. Bad. Marcus Vega.

"Ahhhhhhhhhhhhhhhhhhhhhhhhhhhhhhhhhhhhhh!!!"

I try to catch my breath. My head is throbbing. My throat hurts.

Where the heck am I going to go in the middle of all these trees? I have to go back to the truck. I don't want to. But I have to. I turn back up the hill and make my way to the pickup.

Everyone is still there, waiting, stiff as ever. Nobody says anything. Finally, Charlie pops his head out of the window.

"Hey, why you screaming?" Charlie forms a V-shape with his arms. "Why?"

"Be quiet," I tell him. I've never talked to him like that. He takes it in. My brother is smart. He knows I'm upset. He doesn't care.

"You're Slugworth," he says, sticking out his tongue.

"Slugworth is a good guy, man," I tell him, opening the door.

"H-he is a . . . bad . . . guy . . . in the beginning," he tells me, starting to stutter. "Bleh!"

"Nice," I tell him. "Real mature, man."

"You . . . real . . . mature," he says, stuttering more. My brother stutters when he's upset. He stares at me, trying to get his words out.

"Honey," my mom says to Charlie. "Just leave your brother alone."

And with that, Sergio starts the truck again.

"You know," Darma says, putting her hand on my door, "I never showed your brother our prize toro. He's really a magnificent bull."

Why is she talking to me about her pet bull?

"He doesn't always come to the gates by the stables," she says. "Sometimes he prefers to be out in the fields. Like he's surveying the land. Watching over it. I told your mother you need to see the landscape for yourself to decide what to do."

Is she comparing me to her pet bull?

Darma extends her hand to me. I don't say anything. I just want peace.

She says good-bye to everyone again. We drive off. Everyone is quiet. I look over at the mountains, where my screams have been swallowed by the mist.

SIXTEEN

CHINCHORROS

Sergio says we should stop at a chinchorro after he drops off the plantains.

"Angela and Hilda can check out the place, and maybe you and your mom can talk," Sergio says, looking at us both.

"Yes," she says. "Okay."

I've had a lot of time to think in the silence, but I still don't talk. I'm not sure I have the words right yet. My skin feels prickly, like the spikes from a dragon fruit are rolling up and down my arm. I dig out the rambutan fruit Sergio gave me. It's not as bright orange as it was yesterday. It's turned a little brown. I'm not ready to eat this thing. I put it back in my bag and stare out the window. I feel awful.

We drive through the mountains, toward the little towns where these food-and-drink shacks line the dirt roads. We stop at a farm, and Sergio takes out the cases of plantains to deliver.

"Be right back," he says, leaving the engine running.

Charlie and María play I Spy. My mom just stares out the window. Angela is asleep on Hilda as Hilda quietly rests her head against the car window. I guess they made up or something. I wonder if twins have some kind of internal communication thing where they can apologize to each other without having to say anything. I wish Charlie and my mom could read my mind right now.

Charlie has been calling me Slugworth since we left Darma's. He doesn't say anything else. Just "Slugworth, Slugworth, Slugworth" while he takes in the scenery he missed when he fell asleep on the way up here yesterday.

Sergio returns and then waves to the old guy who just bought the produce. Soon we're back on the road and heading to the highway again. We exit onto a small path, and Sergio pulls over next to a tiny shack. It looks like it's been abandoned for years.

"This is Archie's," Sergio says. "Your dad and I used to hang out here."

We all step out, and Angela and Hilda hurry inside.

My mom and Charlie scope out the scene. Charlie says it looks like a cowboy movie.

"You're right, sweetie," Mom says. "Let's go explore inside."

I still don't understand what has made my mom so adventurous. Back home she's always rushing around, stressing, working double shifts. A few days here and she seems carefree. Like nothing has ever bothered her in her life.

"I've never seen you so excited to do stuff like this, Mom." It's the first thing I say to her after what happened at the farm. Maybe I should have started with something else.

I think Sergio senses that we're going to talk, so he takes Charlie and María inside to meet up with Angela and Hilda.

My mom pauses and looks me in the eyes. "We're together in a different place," she says. "Why shouldn't I feel excited?"

She's right. I can't be mad at her because she wants to be happy. She deserves that.

"Mom, I'm sorry about, you know, about saying that stuff at the farm."

"I'm going to be honest, Marcus. What you said, it hurt. A lot."

"I know," I say. "I just feel angry sometimes."

"And I don't like this new habit of pounding on

things when you get upset. That's not you, Marcus. It's this whole dad thing. It's got you all wound up."

Maybe she's right. Maybe I've just been bottling up this thing about my dad for a long time. I don't know. What I do know is that I messed up. I just want things to be normal again.

"I shouldn't have said those things, Mom. You don't deserve that."

"There are two things in this world that matter to me most. You. And your brother."

I nod.

"Believe it or not, I'm trying to protect you. I just didn't want you to get your hopes up. To get hurt. But Darma made me understand that this is something you need to do. *Have* needed to do. You deserve a chance to talk to him."

She squints her eyes. I can't tell if it's the sun beaming down on her or that she's actually smiling.

"Can I hug you now?" I ask.

She laughs and opens her arms out. "Always."

We hug, and then she puts her arm around my waist and pats my side.

"Come on," she says, leading us to the place Sergio and Hilda call a chinchorro. It's a little trailer with banners hanging from it displaying Coke ads and a sign that says BIENVENIDO.

Charlie and María come out carrying a few cans of

something called Coco Rico. Charlie hands one to me.

"Ready to be a good guy, Slugworth?" he says.

"Yeah, man," I say. "I am."

I open the can and take a sip. The fizz and coconut taste are instantly popular with my taste buds. Another sip turns into a gulp, and soon it's almost gone.

I toss the can in the garbage and head inside with my mom, Charlie, and María.

The place is pretty dark, and even though there are a few lazy fans spinning overhead, it's still pretty humid inside. I move around them, careful not to hit myself. Angela and Hilda chat at the far end of the bar with the lady serving beverages while Sergio talks to a tall guy with chest hair that puffs out from his tank top.

María selects some music from an old jukebox in the corner while my mom and Charlie take seats on one of the high tables in the middle of the room. A few people start grooving on the makeshift dance floor, which inspires Angela and Hilda to leave the bar area. In all this commotion, I don't notice Sergio approach. He says the guy he was talking to is Archie. This must be his place.

"The last time your dad was here was about two years ago," Sergio says.

"Did Archie say what he was doing?"

"He said your dad was trying to set up a chinchorro tour for people visiting Puerto Rico. He asked Archie if he wanted to pay to have his chinchorro listed as one of the stops."

"Seems like a good business," I say. "These places are pretty cool."

"It's a great idea," Sergio says. "Your dad has never had trouble with great ideas."

It seems like my dad tries a whole bunch of things but never seems to finish any of them. Maybe he's been trying to start all these businesses over the years to make some money doing something he's good at. I understand that. But to be gone so long. That's what I don't get.

"I can call Tío Pepe," Sergio says, interrupting my thoughts. "Tía Darma said your dad and him stay in touch occasionally."

"I don't want to have you keep driving us around, Sergio," I say. "You've already helped out a lot."

"Marcus," he says. "You're family. ¿Entiendes?"

I nod. I understand. At least I'm starting to. Sergio gets up and makes a call while I sit silently for a moment. My mom orders more Coco Rico for everyone.

I gulp it down quick again. I tilt the can to try to catch the remaining drops. This. Is. Good.

Sergio sits back down and puts his phone on the table. "Tío Pepe is very excited we're going to visit him in Manatí. He'll try to send word for your dad to come as well. And he's planning on roasting pernil!"

"What's that?" Charlie asks.

"Pork," he says. "It's delicious."

"Remind me," my mom says. "Tío Pepe is the uncle with the house on the beach?"

"Sí," Sergio confirms.

"How many family members do you have?" I ask.

"We. We have a lot," he says. "Tío Pepe is more like a distant cousin, though. But he's family. Like you." Sergio pats my back.

It's still weird to think about.

"We should get going," Sergio says. "It's a bit of a drive."

Tía Darma says Tío Pepe and my dad stay in touch. Maybe he's actually going to come.

Before we leave the chinchorro for good, I take out Danny's camera again. I snap pictures of Archie's old jukebox. I snap pictures of the COCO FRIO sign above the little bar. *Snap. Snap.*

"It will be late by the time we get there," Sergio says. "But you're going to love Tío Pepe's house!"

"Thank you, Sergio," I say.

"I know this is important to you," he says.

"Yeah."

"Can I at least pay for gas money?" My mom tries to hand some cash to Sergio.

"Your money is no good here," he says.

"But the guidebook says the money in Puerto Rico

is exactly the same as the rest of the United States," I say, confused.

"It is," Sergio says, refusing my mom's money. "But this is something I wish to do for my family."

Angela and Hilda approach the truck and take Charlie by the hand.

"I know you need to study, Angela," Hilda says. "We could take a cab back to Tío Ermenio's house when we get to Manatí."

"No way. Abenteuer!" Angela says, squeezing Charlie.

"Adventure!" Charlie says, smiling from ear to ear.

Is my brother speaking German now?

SEVENTEEN
MOONLIGHT PERNIL

We arrive in Manatí and I see a black billboard along the side of the road that reads HACIENDA ESPERANZA RESERVA NATURAL.

"We are in the area," Sergio says. The entire back-seat of the car has fallen asleep. I have too much on my mind to rest.

There are grasslands filled with endless purple flowers whipping by our windows. Up ahead, a huge house sits on a small hill.

"That used to be a sugar plantation," Sergio says. "One of the biggest in the nineteenth century. Much of this area is a nature reserve now."

The sun starts to set across the horizon.

Sergio notices me staring out. "We'll find him, Marcus," he says.

"You think he'll be there?" I ask. "At Tío Pepe's?"

"When we were kids, your dad and I used to run along the beach at Tío Pepe's and pretend we were racing horses. Our feet would splash along the shore as we galloped. He always beat me."

"Really?"

"He has long legs!"

I have long legs too. But I don't do sports.

"Do you know what you're going to tell him when you see him?"

"Not really," I say, because I honestly don't know. I've been so busy this entire time, trying to find him. The thought makes my chest feel funny.

"You'll know what to say," Sergio says. "Just go with your gut."

I nod.

After a few miles, we finally see the blue from the ocean in the distance. Charlie says he's hungry.

"Well, you are in luck, because the pernil should be ready to serve when we get there!"

We twist down a few streets and finally arrive at a small house at the edge of the road.

"Is that it?" I ask, wondering how seven more people are going to fit in such a small house. But then again, we fit seven people into this truck.

"Oh, it's big inside, Marcus," Sergio says, parking the car. "And you can't beat the backyard."

We all tumble out of the car and head to the front door. When we approach, a smell like I've never sniffed before wafts up my nose. I take a deep breath in.

María walks past me through the open door.

"You're not going to knock?" I ask.

"It's family," she says. "No need to knock."

"If you say so . . ."

There is a large painting of a flamingo right as you walk in. Several lamps made out of mason jars filled with light bulbs dangle from the ceiling. I take Charlie's hand, but he wiggles free and walks ahead. I guess he doesn't need me. Meanwhile, Hilda bounces around, inspecting everything, while Angela carefully examines every painting in the bright orange hallway.

"Schau dir das an! Look!" Hilda says, pointing at two swings attached to the ceiling.

"Tío Pepc has eclectic taste," Sergio explains.

Tell me about it. The smell of delicious food keeps the group moving forward. My stomach rumbles. I guess I'm hungry also. Or maybe I'm just nervous that my dad might already be here. We walk through the kitchen and into the large living room. Instead of couches, there are two rowboats stuffed with pillows and a cushion.

María goes to one of the rowboats and lies down,

stretching her legs. "I love these boats," she says. "I used to play pirates on them with my dad when I was little."

Sergio stands by the doorframe and watches his daughter. "She remembers," he says in a hushed tone.

He doesn't say it quietly enough, though, and María overhears him. "Don't start getting sentimental, Papá."

"I won't," he says.

Tío Pepe rushes into the living room, but before I can see what he looks like, he wraps María in a bear hug and doesn't stop kissing her forehead for, like, five minutes. He speaks about a hundred miles an hour.

María seems to melt into her uncle's arms. "Tío Pepe!"

Tío Pepe is wearing a bright orange tank top, cargo shorts, and flip-flops. He sports a gray mustache and a backward baseball cap. He's got, like, twenty shiny bracelets around his wrists. He turns to me and starts rambling in Spanish.

"Sorry," I say. "No hablo español."

Tío Pepe laughs and comes toward me with his arms out wide. "Soy Tío Pepe," he says in a way that sounds kind of like he's singing a really happy song. "I'm so glad you could come!"

He turns to María and makes a gesture like he's measuring me. "¿Cuantos años tiene este niño?"

"Catorce," María says.

"Wow!" Pepe blurts out before continuing in Spanish.

"What did he say?" I ask her.

"He said what everybody says about you, Marcus. You're big for a fourteen-year-old."

We all walk outside, and the smell of food fills the air. Through a walkway of twisting trees, I see cliffs forming around the shimmering dark water ahead. It isn't totally dark yet, so I can see the ocean rumbling against the rocks and the beach up ahead. Charlie, Hilda, Angela, and María run to the shore. A few other people I don't know stand around, drinking cans of Coco Frio and mingling. Apparently, cooking outside in Puerto Rico is an open invitation to everyone in the neighborhood. I scan around but don't recognize my father anywhere.

I follow my brother to the beach. My mom stays behind, talking to Pepe and watching him turn the pork. It really is a whole pig cooking inside a huge metal box covered with a sheet full of coals. I take out my camera. *Snap. Snap.*

My brother inches toward the water. But when the waves crash in, he runs away. I aim the camera. *Snap. Snap. Snap.* As with the fruit and vegetables on Tía Darma's farm, the photos can't fully capture the colors that emerge when the final rays of the sun hit the water. It's warm outside, but there is a breeze rushing against the waves. I watch them ramble against a huge rock a few hundred yards out. The water rises over the rock and tries to push it, but it can't. That's what I feel like most of the time. A rock constantly pushed by millions of drops of water and my brother is on the beach and I'm hoping the water doesn't wet him.

"You know, the Rio Grande de Manatí twists its way out to the Atlantic."

Sergio walks up next to me and watches the waves and the moonlight now taking over the sunlight.

"I used to hike through those mangroves over there," he says, pointing to the twisty trees along the path to the beach. "And my brother and I used to climb up that rock way over there." Sergio points to a large rock at the edge of the water that extends out into the ocean.

"I forgot you had a brother."

"A younger brother," he says. "He's no longer with us."

"Oh," I say. "Sorry."

"He was a captain in the US Army," he says, still looking out to the ocean.

"I didn't know Puerto Ricans could serve."

"Oh yes," he says. "Very much so."

I think about the guy in uniform on the plane. He was on the same flight with us all the way to Puerto Rico. Sergio tells me about a whole bunch of decorated

Puerto Rican men and women who have served in the United States military.

"He served two tours in Afghanistan," Sergio continues. "My parents had already passed away, so it was just him and me. I didn't want him to go."

"Why didn't you just stop him?"

"I tried at first," he says, looking at me. "But I realized it was what he wanted. He wanted to serve."

I look out to the beach at Charlie, who's running around with María, Angela, and Hilda.

"My mom lost her parents when she was twenty-two," I offer.

"Yes, I remember," he says. "Your mother and father bonded over both having lost parents to illness."

"I didn't know that," I say. I wonder why my mom never mentioned it. "Seems like something she would've told me. She hasn't told me a lot about her time with my dad. Up until a couple of days ago I didn't even know I had all this family. I had never even seen the ocean."

Sergio stares for a moment. "Marcus, you've just spoken more than all your words combined over the last three days."

I shrug. "I talk," I say. "I just don't see the point in talking when you don't have to."

Sergio laughs. "Very true."

"So why do you think my mom never told me about

our family down here? Seems like it could have helped."

"I think sometimes we try to protect those we love from hurt. You know what that's like."

"I guess so."

"I know how much you want to protect your brother," Sergio says. "I admire you for that."

I nod. "How do you say 'the sea' in Spanish?" I ask him.

"El mar," he tells me. "Spelled *m-a-r.*"

"That's funny," I tell him.

"Why?"

"That's what Charlie used to call me when he was little."

"Mar?"

"Yeah," I say. "I'm the big, bad, terrible sea, I guess."

Sergio laughs. "You're big," he says. "But you are none of those other things."

I watch the waves calm as they rush to the shore. Maybe nighttime has made them sleepy.

"Come on," Sergio says. "That pork smells like it's ready to be eaten!"

We all shower and change first, just to freshen up after a long day on the road. Tío Pepe gives us some spare clothes and shoes.

"Ponte sandalias," he says, handing me a pair of flip-flops decorated with the Puerto Rican flag. "Too hot for sneakers."

I put the sandals on and they're actually a little big on me. That's a first.

My mom is wearing a summer dress and . . . makeup? Charlie comes out in a tank top, sunglasses, and slicked-back hair. He's strutting around, barefoot.

"Man, put some shoes on," I say, but he ignores me. He hears the music playing outside and starts shaking around like a fool. Three days in Puerto Rico and my brother thinks he's a professional dancer.

By this point, over forty people have gathered in Tío Pepe's backyard. My dad isn't one of them. Almost everyone is dancing, including my mom! She looks over to me and I shake my head.

I'm not dancing.

I rest against a palm tree and watch the whole scene unfold. Where is he?

DAY FOUR

EIGHTEEN
PISA Y CORRE

We end up staying the night at Tío Pepe's house. My mom called Ermenio and let him know so he wouldn't worry. Morning comes and I wake up to Charlie shoving me over and over again.

"Get up, get up!" he says.

"Man, I'm trying to sleep!"

"He emailed!"

My eyes feel like a garage door that's opening and letting in too much light. I feel around the edges of my bed—I'm in one of Tío Pepe's rowboats. My arms and legs are stiff from barely moving a muscle all night. It was scary sleeping in this thing! I was afraid I'd bust the boat open.

"Wake up!" Charlie repeats.

He's not going away, so I swing my legs over the side of the rowboat and break free of the tight space. Charlie shoves my mom's phone in my face.

"Look," he says.

"You took Mom's phone?"

"I was playing Clash of Clams," he says. He loves that game. "The email!"

I take the phone from him and rub my eyes. I can't believe it.

Hello, Marcus,

If you are all still in Puerto Rico when you get this, come to the Maravilla Resort and Residencies in Dorado.

I'll be working there.

—M

I read over the email several times. Then I re-read the emails I sent him. Almost every place I was at on this trip is in there. He doesn't mention any-thing about them. Maybe he prefers to speak in person.

My mom walks into the living room and watches

me reread the email. She doesn't say anything. Charlie bounces into the rowboat and starts humming.

"There's no telling, where we going," he sings, moving side to side. "There's no way or even knowing."

"That's not how the song goes, man," I tell him, giving him a gentle shove. He laughs and rolls around in the rowboat.

"Well, there you have it," my mom finally says. "He responded."

I nod.

"The hotel isn't far," Sergio says. "About twenty-five minutes away."

"Did you know he was there?" I ask my mom.

She shakes her head. "No, honey."

"This hotel job must be a new thing," Sergio offers. "In any case, we'll go. Right, Mel?"

"Sure," Mom says. But she doesn't sound totally sure. Just sure enough.

"Okay," I tell them. I suddenly feel excited and nervous at the same time.

"Tío Pepe went to get eggs and bacon for breakfast," she says. "We can head out after we eat."

After three days of searching, I'm finally going to see my dad for the first time in ten years. I don't have the same feeling I had when we first got here, or even yesterday. Like, I don't know, maybe this isn't such a great idea.

My mom must notice that my mind is spinning, because she says, "It'll be fine, sweetie. It's time."

I nod and I wonder what my dad will say to me first.

⊕⊕⊕

We all eat breakfast and thank Tío Pepe for another great meal and a wonderful stay. He tells me to keep the flip-flops. I don't mind. It's been really humid these last few days, and my feet feel kind of free walking around in sandals. Plus, I kind of like the Puerto Rican flags painted on them.

"We should have come here years ago," my mom suddenly offers. "I'm sorry for that."

"Don't be sorry, Mom," I tell her. "You're doing the best you can."

"We're going to do things differently when we get back home," she says. "No more late-night shifts. No more dinners alone."

I nod. "And maybe Dad will help us out," I offer.

She smiles and pats my shoulder. "Come on," she says. "Let's go see him."

We are about to head out of Tío Pepe's house when we hear a loud *POP*. We all step outside to find Sergio fanning the hood of the truck, which has smoke curling out.

"We may need to wait a little bit," he says, frantically

trying to clear the smoke. "It appears our truck has popped a gasket."

The lime-green pickup that has taken us around the island lets out one last puff before going completely silent. Sergio gives it a kick and then quickly apologizes to it. He paces around while cursing, and then apologizes to us for cursing.

Charlie carefully leans over the truck and starts blowing on it. He looks at Sergio and shakes his head. "Nope, it's dead."

Sergio rubs his sweaty head. His concerned look morphs into a slight chuckle followed by a full-blown laugh. Everyone joins in, but we're not sure what we're laughing about. Sergio walks around the car and puts his arm around Charlie.

"An excellent prognosis, Doctor."

Charlie beams at being called a doctor. Everyone continues to laugh it off. I stop laughing. My dad actually wants to see us, and now we can't get to him.

"Let's call the mechanic," Sergio suggests. "At least we're close to town."

"Let's call him," I tell my mom.

"Who, a mechanic?" Mom replies.

"No, Dad. Call him at the hotel. See if he'll come pick us up."

"What about everyone else, Marcus? They don't have transportation now."

I look around. I wouldn't want to leave them. They're part of this journey now. But I also can't wait around to fix the car or stay here another night. We leave for Springfield tomorrow.

"Doesn't Tío Pepe have a car?" I ask.

Sergio says that Pepe doesn't drive. He says I should try to stay positive, but what is there to be positive about? We've come all this way only to stop short of the finish line. I ask if Ermenio can pick us up, but Sergio says he doesn't drive either.

"Does any old man drive in Puerto Rico?" I suddenly blurt out.

"Hey," my mom says. "That's not a very nice thing to say. Everyone has been so helpful to us, Marcus. Chill out, okay?"

I lean against the wall and fold my arms. I know I should chill out like my mom says, but it's all just so unfair. Why did the truck have to break down on our last day in Puerto Rico?

"A bus!" My brother interrupts my train of thought. "Let's take a little bus!"

"The buses don't run around here, Charlie," María says. "It's mostly in San Juan."

"No, the little bus! The little ones!"

Charlie takes out a map and spreads it out on the floor. He points at an ad for a mini bus service.

"A pisa y corre! Of course," María says. "These are little buses that drive through the towns. They're like taxis, only you share them with other people. Brilliant, Charlie!"

Charlie beams.

All that research he did before we left is paying off. My brother, the problem-solver.

"I'll return for the truck tomorrow," Sergio says.

"I'm coming with you, Papi." María stands up and walks toward us. "Let's go find their dad."

"You don't have to come," I say.

"I know I don't *have* to," she says. "But I *want* to."

Sergio starts to get all teary-eyed, but María stops him.

"No empieces," she says. It sounds like she's telling him not to start with the mushy stuff again.

"Let's go!" says Angela.

"Let's call Papa to tell him first," Hilda says. "Er macht sich sorgen."

Angela nods. "Ja," she says. "Good idea."

We all look at each other, confused, until Angela translates.

"Our father worries. He likes us to call often."

Hilda calls their dad and tells him something in German. She keeps nodding.

"Ja, Papa," she says, then hands the phone over to her sister. Angela takes it and talks with her dad.

"He was very happy to hear me calling him," Hilda says. "I always let my sister do the talking."

Angela hangs up with her dad and walks over to us.

"Wir kommen mit!"

Hilda smiles and looks at us. "Angela says we're coming with!"

María checks where the little pisa y corre bus is located.

"It's in la plaza," she says. "There should be a few of them. They don't leave until they are completely full."

We all say good-bye to Tío Pepe. He gives us each a kiss on the cheek. I give one back because that's what you do around here. We walk down the sidewalk toward the plaza. Our travel companions, my mom, my brother, and I march through the small sidewalks almost in a perfect single file. Like an invisible line connects us all. I take out my camera. *Snap. Snap. Snap.* We pass a little place that looks like a chinchorro. I think about the word "chinchorro." It was difficult for me to say a few days ago. Now it rolls around my tongue like a Tic Tac.

The first thing María does when we get to the plaza is look for the little buses. She moves around the people peddling hats and jewelry. Some lady offers my mom hair accessories. There are smells wafting in every direction. Pineapple, fish, various herbs.

I take a few pictures. *Snap. Snap. Snap.*

"Mira, Papá," María says. "This is a good market for us to sell fruits and vegetables."

"You want to keep doing that?"

"Why wouldn't I?"

"But you're leaving," Sergio says. "To college. In Florida."

"I'm going to study agricultural engineering, Papá!" María exclaims. "Where did you think I was going to go after? To a farm in Montana?"

"You want to come back to Puerto Rico, to help me?" Sergio walks close to María. I can tell he's about to lose it.

"Don't get emotional, ¡por favor!"

"I won't," he says. "Promise."

María is all business, but I can tell how much she loves her dad. She finds a little bus and asks the driver if he has room and if he can make a stop in Dorado at the hotel where my dad works.

The driver says yes and everyone climbs in. There are already a few people inside, waiting patiently. A few older ladies sitting by the window watch us.

My mom sits next to one of them. The lady is reading a newspaper and immediately starts talking to Mom in Spanish. I think she's talking about an article because she keeps pointing at it. My mom tries to answer her in Spanish, but she has a hard time. She nods and agrees, although I'm not sure what she's agreeing to.

"What is she saying?" I ask.

"I think she's talking about the identity of Puerto Rico and how it's up to the people to maintain it."

The lady talks to us about her concerns about the high unemployment rate, the recent school closings, the island's debt. It's cool that she's trusting us with her ideas, and it seems like she wants to hear what we think. Twice she leans over and pats my mom's forearm. She has a habit of picking at her teeth when she talks and then pulling on her chin when she needs a moment to pause. I ask her if I can take her photo, and she says yes. She's someone I want to remember.

The little bus starts up. My mom hands Sergio some money for the fare.

"I'm thirsty," Charlie says.

"Now?"

"Yes," he says.

"I'll go get him something," I tell Mom. "There's a stand over there."

I step out of the little van and go to the stand across the street to buy two cans of Coco Frio. I look back to the van and ask everyone else if they want anything. They all say no. I buy two drinks and start back across the street.

"¡Un chocolate!" the old lady yells from the window. "Por favor."

"Um, okay." I say, and head back to the stand to buy the lady a chocolate.

The pisa y corre rumbles to life with loud music and

several honks. This bright canary-yellow bus lets out one long, steady honk before starting off.

"Come on, Marcus!" Sergio says. "Once it starts it won't stop!"

I bolt to the little bus, but it's already driving off.

"Come on!" my mom says, sticking her head out of the tiny window. She turns back inside and I see her yelling at the driver to stop.

Seriously? He couldn't wait? I start running, but I'm getting tired. My dad used to pretend he was a horse running on the beach, and I can't jog a few hundred feet to catch up to this little bus! In all fairness, I only run once a year in PE. I can't believe the driver isn't stopping!

And then the bus really takes off.

"Mom!" My legs are long, but I'm barely able to keep up.

"Hurry up, Marcus!" she says.

"Mom!" I say, frantically trying to keep pace with the bus.

My mom's face turns pale when she sees the pisa y corre getting farther and farther away from me. "Marcus, hurry up!"

I'm running out of breath. I can't keep up with the tiny moving bus now that it's speeding faster and faster. Seriously? I can't catch up to a tiny little bus? Why aren't my long legs helping me right now? I'm totally starting a workout routine when I get back home.

"Mom!"

"Marcus, you have to run!"

I'm running out of air. I start slowing down. The camera around my neck dangles like it's about to give up also.

"Marcus! Hurry up, slowpoke!"

I stop panting and look up long enough to see Charlie sticking his head out of the pisa y corre, screaming at the top of his lungs for me to hurry.

"We're leaving you!" he yells again.

My feet ignore my lungs, and I take off in a sprint. The reggaeton music coming from the pisa y corre is both incredibly irritating and unbelievably catchy and motivating as I run. Hilda sticks her head out of the other window to cheer me on. My mom tries to get the driver to stop, but he shakes his head. The jerk. I'm running out of air. Charlie's voice drowns out everything else.

"Hurry. Up. Slowpoke."

My brother, the motivational speaker.

Finally, enough of our group complains and gets the driver to listen. The bus skids to a stop and kicks up dust and rocks all over me. The door slides open.

"¡Apurate!" the driver barks.

I hop in and move past my mom, who is now sitting in the middle row. I barely have time to drag myself to a seat when the driver speeds off again. He starts talking to us like he didn't almost just leave me behind.

"¡Qué lindo día!"

Did he just say what a beautiful day we're having? Seriously?

I grab the safety bar above me and hold on for dear life. This guy is reckless. The old lady next to us reaches her hand out.

"¿Y el chocolate?" she asks.

Great. I forgot the lady's chocolate. Instead, I offer her my Coco Frio. She takes it and slurps it down before handing it back to me.

"You can keep it," I say.

The people inside congratulate me on my victory/ near-death experience on this wild little bus driving a hundred miles an hour through the Puerto Rican countryside. My brother turns to face me in his seat and pats my shoulder.

"Man, you're slow," he says.

I take his head and put it under my armpit. "How does my sweat smell?"

"Ah! Gross!"

He pulls away. His glasses slide to the edge of his nose as he wipes his face.

The bus makes a few more dangerous stops and a few people get on or off. About twenty-five minutes later, the country gives way to a few buildings in the distance. I see a sign that says DORADO.

"Esa es nuestra parada," Sergio says, indicating

this is our stop.

The little bus slows down and finally comes to a halt.

We're circling another plaza, only this one has taller buildings that feel more like the ones in San Juan. The driver says something in Spanish and we all exit the bus.

"We need to get a taxi to the hotel," Sergio says. "The pisa y corre doesn't run to the hotels."

Angela, Hilda, María, Sergio, my mom, Charlie, and I walk to the sidewalk at the edge of the town. The bus driver turns the bus off and takes out his newspaper while he waits for new passengers to load in.

The old lady waves good-bye. "Bendiciones," she says.

"Gracias," my mom replies, and then turns to me. "She's blessing us."

"Wish she could have blessed the driver so he would have slowed down," I tell her.

A few cars pass by and I can see immediately that this isn't the same sort of beachside neighborhood where we left Tío Pepe an hour ago. The cars here are shiny and new, like the cars parked in the Cherry Hill neighborhood back home. Only the streets aren't covered in snow, and the trees here are palms, not fir or pine. There are fancy restaurants, cafés, and stores. Men walk around in shiny suits, and many of them talk on cell phones. This place has a very different vibe. I decide I'm going to wait until we see my dad to take more pictures. It'll be a fitting conclusion to the trip. Then I'll put them together and show Danny all the places we went in search of my dad. Danny will like that.

"The little airport in Dorado was a military landing strip in the fifties," Sergio says. He really likes talking like a tour guide. "My brother loved Puerto Rican military history. Come on. There's a taxi stand close by."

If my dad works in this neighborhood, he definitely has money to help us out. I wonder what he looks like now. The picture on his ID looks just like me, but that was taken years ago. Does he like to read? Does he like movies? Which ones? I hope he remembers us. He barely met Charlie. Okay, I need to chill. No sense in getting all nervous.

We get to the taxi stop and wait for a minivan to pull up. Sergio argues with the taxi driver that we'll all fit in the car just fine and that we're going to the Maravilla Beach Resort. The taxi driver doesn't care. He doesn't want us all cramming into his taxi.

María walks over to the driver and hands him some money. She tells him to let us ride. He counts the extra ten bucks and opens the door for us. María steps in first, followed by Angela, Hilda, my mom, and Charlie. Sergio piles in last and tells me to sit up front with the driver.

I don't want to, but I know I have to. There's no way I can fit back there with everyone. Inside, the taxi reeks of really powerful cologne. It makes me nauseous. I'm seriously about to pass out. I hear María coughing a little and Hilda laughing while Angela hushes her. In the end, Angela can't help laughing also.

"It stinks in here," Charlie blurts out.

"¿Qué dijo? No lo entiendo. What did he say?"

The guy doesn't understand my brother.

I'm about to clarify when Hilda answers, "He loves music!"

All of a sudden the guy turns up the radio.

Great. Now I'm light-headed *and* my eardrums are about to pop.

We drive through town and into a neighborhood. We continue down a road and finally reach a set of iron gates with an emblem on each gate. We pull up and a security guard comes out. The taxi driver says we're being dropped off because we have a meeting with Mr. Vega.

"Actually, he's our dad," I say, surprising myself.

The security guard looks inside the taxi. "Are you staying in the hotel, señora?" he says to my mom.

"No," she says. "My sons are here to see their father." My mom points to my brother and me.

"And who are these people?"

"They're our family," Charlie says, smiling at the security guard.

The guard looks at him for a moment, then at the rest of us. "I'll need all of your names."

He takes out a notebook, and after about ten minutes, he opens the massive gates and lets us in. The huge stone columns lining the road that lead up to the hotel look like they belong in a fairy-tale palace.

"Wow!" Hilda says, then blurts out something in German.

"'Rich' is one thing to call this place," Angela replies.

I open the window to look at the bright red flowers with yellow flecks in the middle lining the long driveway.

There are several gardens with gigantic palm trees lined up along the whole road. There are two-, three-, and four-story buildings on each side of the perfectly paved path. Up ahead at the circular entrance is the biggest fountain I have ever seen, and a building that straight up looks like a castle. We drive around the fountain and into a high-ceilinged entryway. Several men dressed in white and wearing little caps open car doors. They look like they're from a spy movie. The taxi driver pulls up to the entrance. One of the guys in white opens my door and I step out. My dad is somewhere inside this massive place.

NINETEEN
HOTEL MARAVILLA

"Bienvenidos," the guy in white says. We make eye contact, and by the look on his face, I can tell he's thinking the same thing I am: What the heck are we doing here?

We walk through the enormous double doors. Enormous even for me. There is a chandelier in the middle of the entrance and a seating area on each side.

"Wow," Charlie says. "He works here?"

"I guess so," my mom replies.

Sergio, Angela, Hilda, and María fan out.

"We'll meet back here at three thirty," Sergio says. "Good luck, boys!"

Sergio is always so positive and helpful (and way emotional about María). I wonder if having lost his brother and his parents when he was younger made him care more about people. Like if maybe he wants those around him to feel welcome and safe. Mom says I'm a heat giver. I think Sergio wouldn't mind the cold so much either.

My mom takes our hands and we start toward the reception area. She asks about Mr. Marcus Antonio Vega. The guy takes a look at us and wrinkles his nose like we're the worst-smelling people he has ever gotten a whiff of.

"He is in meetings, señora," the guy huffs. "He's very busy."

I check myself out in the large mirror behind him. I look like I fought a grizzly bear in the mud. I ran after that little bus for, like, half a mile, and the dirt from the country mixed with my sweat is now caked all over my body and feet. Even my Puerto Rican flag sandals look dirty. Nice way to meet your dad for the first time in ten years.

Charlie watches the TV screens in a bar area behind the reception desk. Some basketball game is on. He moves closer, like the TV has put a spell on him or something.

"Charlie, don't stand so close to the TV, man. You're going to get a headache."

He waves his hand dismissively at me and continues watching. He doesn't seem nervous to be here at all. My mom asks the guy behind the desk if he can page my father. He grudgingly picks up the phone and starts dialing. It annoys me that he thinks he's better than us.

I walk over to Charlie, who hasn't taken his eyes off the screen. His neck tilts back because the TV is too high for him to see level.

"At least sit down, man."

Charlie looks at me briefly, then at the cushy chair facing the TV. He walks backward to it and plops down. It's some team from Puerto Rico playing basketball with some other team from Puerto Rico. I don't get why he cares about this game.

"Your dad is finishing a meeting," my mom says behind me.

"Did the guy at the front desk call him?"

"No, I just saw him."

My heart skips a couple of beats and my stomach flops. It's the way I felt on the two flights it took to get here.

"Where?"

"Over there," she says, pointing about one hundred feet from where Charlie sits.

There's a guy smiling with some people at the table. He's wearing a brown tailored suit with no tie.

I notice he's not wearing socks and his shoes are really shiny. His hair is combed perfectly, and he barely has any facial hair. I don't see the resemblance. This guy is totally clean-cut. He looks nothing like the picture on the ID.

"How do you know that's him?"

"I was married to him, Marcus. That's your father."

"But he doesn't look anything like the ID."

"He had more hair. And back then he didn't care about what he wore or who he impressed."

This guy seems like he cares about how he looks. I catch myself in another mirror—mud-streaked face and all. Why are there so many mirrors in this place?

"Honey? Are you okay?"

We came all this way to talk to a guy who I thought was supposed to look like me. Maybe sound like me. Maybe even act like me. This guy sitting at the table looks nothing like I do. He looks like he would live in the Cherry Hill neighborhood. Like he would send his kids to the best private schools. Except he hasn't.

This guy isn't my dad. My dad is the guy in the ID. A guy who loved growing vegetables and being outdoors. A guy who started new businesses all over the place. Who loved to run on the beach with his cousin. Who visited family members. Who would be happy we've spent time with them. Gotten to know them. A guy who would be thrilled we came to visit him. A guy who would apologize to my mom and help out his kids.

"Marcus, honey," my mom says. She takes a tissue from her bag and wipes my cheeks. I don't take my eyes off the guy at the table.

"Sweetie, let's get some water and sit down. Okay?"

My mom takes my hand and guides me to a seat next to my brother. He pats it and tells me to watch the game. My mom grabs us some water from the bar. I drink it fast. My throat is dry. My eyes sting. My head hurts.

"We can do this another time, sweetie. We can come back to Puerto Rico."

"No," I say. "I mean, yes, I want to come back. But no, Mom. Everyone has been all around this island with us, looking for him. Looking for him because *I* wanted to find him. I need to do this."

I stare at the game on TV. I have no idea which team is which or who is winning. I just don't want to look at my mom or Charlie. The guy at the table keeps popping in and out of my head. I close my eyes, trying to erase his image. Why did I come here? Was it for my brother? My mom? Or was it really just for me? Was I trying to understand something that really had no explanation? My dad left me. He left us. And he turned into someone who is nothing like us.

I finally get out of my head when I hear a man say, "Hola, Mel." It's him.

"Hi, Marcus," my mom says. Her tone is reserved and she keeps it short.

There he is. Standing right next to us. I can tell he's looking at me, but I don't turn to face him. My eyes are fixed on Puerto Rican basketball.

"Hello, Marcus," he says.

Charlie turns to him.

"And this is Carlitos?" the man asks.

"Charlie," my mom corrects.

"Hello, Charlie," he says.

Charlie scoots back in his seat and stares at his shoes.

"I got our son's messages. His many, many, many messages. The trip was okay?"

"Yeah," my mom says.

"How is Tío Ermenio?"

"Good. He hasn't touched your room. It's exactly as you left it. He hopes you'll come back one day."

"We always had so much fun with Tío Ermenio, remember?"

My mom nods.

"You're leaving tomorrow?"

My mom nods again.

If I don't get up and say something now, I'll never get another chance. I know I'll regret it.

"Your mom says you want to talk to me," he says, smiling.

I nod.

"Why don't we take a tour of the hotel and we can talk? Does that sound good? Charlie, do you want to see the big pool?"

Charlie turns to my dad and smiles. "Yes."

"Good, let's walk to the pool first. Do you have swimming shorts?"

"We brought a small travel bag," I suddenly say. My throat is dry. I need another glass of water.

"Okay," he says. "Would you like to go to the pool?"

"I don't really swim," I say. "Never learned."

"You didn't give him swimming lessons, Mel?"

My mom glares at him.

"It's cold in Springfield," I tell him. "And the outdoor pool in the community center hasn't been open for years."

"It *is* cold over there!" he says. "*Way* too cold for me."

My mom mutters something under her breath, but I don't catch it. My dad looks at my shoulders and sees I have goose bumps from the air conditioning. I'm not used to fake cold.

"You're friolento, just like your old man, huh?" My dad points to my goose bumps and laughs. "Remember how cold I used to get in the winter, Mel?"

"Yep," my mom says. "I still live there, remember?"

This conversation is not going well.

"So where's the pool?" I ask.

My dad pats my shoulder and extends his hand to Charlie. "Follow me."

Charlie takes my dad's hand and together we walk around the enormous hotel as my mom stays several paces behind. She's trying to give us some space, but I don't think she's willing to hand us over to our dad completely. My dad swipes at a few doors with a card. They open to rooms with even more elaborate designs. There is a ballroom, a fitness center, even a library. This place has everything.

"So did you ever open your restaurant, or start your tour company of the chinchorros?" I ask, wondering what he does in this fancy hotel.

"Have you been stalking me or something? Ha, I'm just kidding," he says, then winks and smiles. I don't smile back. "Those businesses," he says, "weren't really for me."

It's strange hearing him say that. All I've heard about is how much he loved farming and the outdoors.

"So what do you do now?" I ask.

My dad tells me he started working for the resort about nine months ago.

"Total game changer," he says. "A whole lot cleaner than shaking dirt off fruit."

"I just thought, you know, you wanted to start those chinchorro tours. What about the farm you were going to start with Sergio?"

"Sergio is a good guy, but he never strikes out on his own. He's always asking Darma for advice. I take action. Anyway, that life is too slow for me," he says. "Puerto Rico's tourism industry is way more lucrative than its agriculture."

He continues to tell us about the hotel and its history. He says this property used to be an orphanage run by nuns.

"Can you imagine how incredible it would have been to be an orphan living in this place? It would be like Puerto Rican Annie in Daddy Warbucks's home!"

"Right," I say, trying to agree with him, although why would anyone *want* to be an orphan?

We go through another secured door and enter a courtyard that has the largest pool I've ever seen in my life. A fountain shoots water into the pool.

"I want to go," Charlie says. "I want to go in the pool."

My dad pauses. "What did you say?"

"He said he wants to go in the pool," I tell him. My dad doesn't understand Charlie at all. He keeps bending over to try to pick up what he's saying. Then he looks at me to translate.

"Oh, well, did your mom bring your bathing suit, my

friend?" my dad asks Charlie. "Because you can't swim in your underwear."

I think this is supposed to be a joke, but nobody laughs. Charlie walks over to the edge of the pool and puts his hand in.

"Be careful, man," I say, walking toward him.

"I won't fall like Augustus Gloop!"

"What did he say?" my dad asks again.

"He's talking about the kid who fell into the chocolate river in *Willy Wonka*."

"Oh," he says. "So do you like the place? It's beautiful, ¿no?"

"Yeah," I say. "It's really nice."

"A place you could maybe visit? Plus, I work here now. You could use vacation weeks, or maybe trade points for a larger suite."

"What?"

"You said you like this place, ¿no?"

"Yeah, it's fine, I guess."

"And your brother likes it?"

Charlie splashes water in the pool and cracks up every time the splashes reach my mom, who has moved a bit closer to us now.

"You should ask her," my dad says, watching my mom. "Ask her if she'd like to purchase a time-share here."

"Huh?" What is he asking?

He takes out a small notepad from his jacket pocket and starts scribbling some numbers down. He shows them to me.

"It's really not that expensive," he says. "And this would be your home base. Where I work. We could see each other at least one week a year, more depending on the package your mom chooses."

Oh, I know what's happening. A sudden electric charge runs through me. My dad is trying to sell me a time-share. He's only showing us around this gigantic place that feels cold and empty inside because he's trying to sell us on it. My head spins.

He continues to talk about the architecture and the tennis courts and the square footage of the two-bedroom suites and how great it all is. Finally, I gather my focus. I watch him carefully. He's about to speak again, but I interrupt him in the middle of his bit about twenty-four-hour concierge service.

"Why did you leave?" I say, my voice trembling.

He seems shocked. I just interrupted the sales pitch he's memorized, and it seems like he doesn't know what to do. He remains silent for a moment.

"It's complicated, Marcus," he tells me.

"You know what's complicated?" I start. "Feeling like you have to keep everything together all the time." The words are almost ahead of my thoughts, but I don't stop. "Help out with money, take care of my brother, make sure my mom doesn't feel too guilty. It's tough."

"I'm sorry, Marcus," he says.

"And it isn't easy at school," I continue. My heart beats faster with every word. "It's lonely being the biggest kid. Being feared just because of my size. Feeling invisible on the inside because all anyone ever sees is the outside. They just assume I'm a monster. They call me that. Over and over again. It's not easy. And my brother deserves a chance just like everyone else. And I'm probably going to get expelled from school and Charlie is going to be left alone to fend for himself and my mom will have to keep working extra shifts just to cover the basic bills. And in all of this . . . *where* have you been?"

"You're going to get expelled?" he says suddenly, acting concerned. "What did you do?"

"I punched a kid for saying something about my brother." I can feel the blood rushing to my cheeks.

"You punched a kid? Marcus, being expelled is a pretty big deal."

"You're going to be my father now?" I feel myself stepping closer to him. "Just a second ago you were selling me a one-bedroom suite."

"It was a two—" He doesn't finish. "One-bedroom, two-bedroom—who's keeping track?" he says, backing away like the kids at school.

"Where have you been, man?"

My dad tells me he was young. He didn't know how to be a father, much less to a kid like Charlie. It makes the blood rush to my neck and cheeks and then down to my fists, but he continues to talk.

"An opportunity came up to start a business in Puerto Rico," he says. "It was a pharmaceutical start-up in Toa Baja."

"And what about working in Pennsylvania? Where your *wife* and *kids* live?"

"There was no way to earn enough money there," he says. "Marcus, if a business is failing, you find another one. Why doesn't *anybody* understand that?"

With each excuse he gives, I become less angry.

I realize what everyone has been telling me all along. "They do understand," I finally tell him. "But they also know that sometimes the necessary thing isn't always the easiest."

"Ay, Díos mío, you've been spending too much time with Tía Darma," he says, shaking his head.

My mom and Charlie have been standing there the entire time. My mom doesn't say anything when my dad finally finishes talking. But Charlie does.

"You broke the rules!"

"What?" my dad asks.

Charlie steps close to him, and I swear he's trying to make every syllable come out as perfectly as he can.

"It's all there, black and white, clear as crystal! You

stole fizzy-lifting drinks, so you get NOTHING! You lose! Good day, sir!"

Charlie steps back, digs into my mom's purse, pulls out his crumpled Wonka hat, and puts it on his head. It flops over, but he doesn't care. He stares down my dad, his hands on his hips.

My mom tries to hold in a laugh, but she ends up snorting.

"Did he just?"

"Yeah," I tell her.

"Oh man," she says. "That one is going down as one of the all-time greatest Charlie moments."

"Definitely," I say.

My dad looks confused.

"You stole fizzy-lifting drinks, man," I tell him. "You shouldn't have done that."

"What are you talking about?"

Out of the corner of my eye, I see Angela, María, Hilda, and Sergio being let into the pool area by another guy dressed just like my father.

"There they are!" Hilda says, then thanks the guy.

"Sorry, we're not in the market for a time-share," María says, handing the guy back his business card. The guy tries to talk about the highlights of the property.

"I said, no. Thank you." María stares at the guy. He backs off. I wouldn't mess with María. She has that same *I might have to kill a cow* look that Darma has. The guy scurries off and leaves them poolside. They walk toward us from one of the pool bars.

"Hola, primo," Sergio says.

"Sergio," my dad says.

"Are you all set?" Sergio asks me.

I nod, but I have one last thing to say.

"I always thought I wanted to see you," I tell my dad. "To let you meet my brother, who is the coolest kid in the world. But you never answered. You never even tried. I just want you to know that you're not the hero in this story." I point to my mom. "She's my hero."

The anger rushing over me cools. I've only punched one person in my life. I'm not sure I ever want to punch someone again. It didn't feel good. It hurt. I could do it to him, though. Nobody would blame me. But I don't. Instead, I offer him something.

I dig into my pocket and hand him his Pennsylvania driver's license.

"Here you go," I tell him. "I don't need to hold on to this."

And like that, I put my father away forever.

"*You're* the hero, sweetheart," my mom says, and kisses me on the cheek.

"Everyone!" Charlie says, putting his hand up for high fives as we walk back inside the hotel. "I am the hero. Marcus is my sidekick."

I put my arm around his shoulders.

"Come on, show-off. Let's get out of here."

Angela, Hilda, María, Sergio, my mom, and Charlie surround me. They hug me and stay close. Now I know what Danny and those other kids must feel when I walk them. Protected.

TWENTY
FAMILIA MONSTRUO

As we wait on the curb for a taxi, I realize I'm hungry. I reach into my bag and dig out the rambutan Sergio gave me back at Darma's farm. It's not bright orange anymore. It looks like it's gone bad. Sergio notices.

"It's still good, you know? You just have to peel off the skin."

He hands me his pocketknife, and I carefully slice it open. The little white ball is inside. I scoop it out and take a bite, careful not to chew through the seed. The sweet and sour flavors tickle my tongue. My mom is right. This is delicious.

We wait for the taxi, laughing and making jokes.

"Where to now?" I say, because really, after all the

driving we've done around Puerto Rico, I have no idea.

"Now we go grab some food and then we go home."

"Thank you for sticking with us, Sergio," my mom says.

"Melissa, this is what we do for family."

María bribes another taxi driver and we all get in. I don't feel cramped anymore, though.

I lean my head against the seat and roll down the window. I let the warm air wash over me. I take out my camera again. *Snap. Snap. Snap.* Pictures of everyone in the car on our way back to Old San Juan.

"It's too hot! Roll up the window! I need AC!" Charlie pushes the front seat to get my attention.

My brother, the mood crusher.

I thought about what happened. My mom knew all along. She knew my dad would be that way. Everyone did. My mom knew he had moved on to another life long ago. But she also knew that I needed to go. Darma helped her understand that. Tío Ermenio is right. Darma is tough and really smart. And she's real. I like that.

We pass a billboard advertising a battery.

EL CLIMA ES IMPREDECIBLE—PREPÁRATE

It's something about the climate. It's something about being prepared. We pass another one. It's a company I don't recognize.

"Lugar" means "place." I know because I heard María say it in the car on the way to the farm. "Momento" has to mean "moment." "Ahora" is "now," or "time." I don't remember.

We drive on, and I read more signs that are mostly in Spanish. It's like another country out here. Except it's not. It's an island in the middle of the ocean where people speak English and Spanish and sometimes a mix of both. It's full of contradictions. The people here can serve in the US military but can't vote for president. How does that make sense? Where they play the same sports as we do back in Springfield. Have the same passport. The same currency. It's part of the same country. It's a place where a Puerto Rican living in Chicago can invent a sandwich that reminds people of their culture, and a tall kid living in a small town in Pennsylvania can learn he has a culture and family he can claim. I came here to find my dad. But I didn't find him. I found something else.

My mom knows we'll return. Return to the farm in the clouds. To the family we found. She knows. We all do.

After a long drive, we enter the cobblestone streets of Old San Juan again. Everyone takes out money to pay the taxi driver when we reach Tío Ermenio's place, but Sergio refuses my mom's money again.

"No, you keep it."

My mom tries to insist, but María, Angela, and Hilda block her. The cab driver is patient while we figure it out, and then zips off. We stare at the old building with no doorknob, and I instantly feel warm inside. It's the feeling you get when you're glad to be somewhere.

"What a trip, huh?" my mom says, stretching. "I'm sorry you had to experience that one bad spot, sweetie." No bad spots, I think. Just doors that needed to be closed and new ones I'm so glad we opened.

DAY FIVE

TWENTY-ONE
LIKE ALL THINGS

Charlie doesn't want to leave the next morning after breakfast and, to be honest, I don't either. My mom hugs and thanks Tío Ermenio.

"Now you have to come back sooner," he says. "I hardly saw you!"

"I know!" my mom says. "I promise we'll be back soon. Maybe even this summer!"

"This is your home," Tío Ermenio says.

My mom got close to him on this trip. I can tell by the way she kept calling him to tell him we were okay on the road.

Next, she turns to María. "You can stay with us whenever you want," my mom says.

"Thank you," she says.

"We're not too far from New Jersey. There are amazing tomatoes there!"

"In New Jersey?" María asks.

"Oh, there are places that will surprise you," my mom says. "Jersey is one of them."

María laughs.

"Maybe we'll fly from Florida to visit you in Pennsylvania?" Sergio says.

"What do you mean, Papá?"

"After I visit you in college, maybe we can take a trip to Springfield?"

"You're afraid of flying."

"Ah, I think I'll manage. Right, Marcus?"

"Not gonna lie, Sergio. Flying is scary," I tell him.

"Marcus!" Mom says.

"What? I'm serious; it's nerve-racking." I look at the old building with no doorknobs. "But totally worth it."

Angela braids Hilda's hair at the foot of the stairs and Hilda blows kisses at us.

"Wir werden euch vermissen," she says.

"Hilda says we'll miss you," Angela says.

Hilda nods while Angela finishes the braids, and then gets up to hug us. "Be well, my handsome Marcus," she whispers to me.

I nod and I think I blush a little.

Sergio puts his arm on my shoulder. "Oh, Marcus,"

he says, bringing me closer. "I'll be sending you the bill for my broken-down truck."

He winks and I laugh.

After our last good-byes, we all hop in a cab and head to the airport. My mom promises we'll return, and I believe her. We all do.

***

We finally land in Philly after a long day of travel. The airport is quiet. It doesn't sound like Puerto Rico. It's like someone hit the mute button. We walk outside, and the brisk air and gray sky remind me that we're back home. Puerto Rico is humid. The heat makes you open up. Literally, your pores sweat constantly. Here it's the opposite. The cold tightens. You have to keep things closed. Bundled.

My mom sounds refreshed. She sounds like she is ready to take on the world.

"First thing I'm doing on Monday is meeting with Principal Jenkins. He has to accommodate us. He must."

My mom, the fighter.

For dinner, we order takeout. We sit around the kitchen table and munch on black beans and rice with steak from the Cuban restaurant in town. We don't have a Puerto Rican restaurant in our neighborhood.

The food from this place is good. Not as good as the stuff I ate back in PR, but it's not bad.

Charlie helps clean up after dinner, which is a total shocker.

"Whoa! Maybe we should send you to Darma's farm once a month?"

Charlie says he wants to go back tomorrow.

"Not so soon, honey. We will, though."

Charlie finishes washing up, takes a bath by himself, and gets into his pajamas. He is happy because he knows he's going back to school on Monday. He wants to tell all his friends about his trip to Puerto Rico.

"They're going to be so jealous," he says while I tuck him in. He wrinkles his nose and holds out his hand. I bring my head down to his and our noses touch.

"Nose kiss," he says, rubbing his nose against mine.

"Mr. Wonka," I tell him, smiling back.

"Ha! Mr. Wonka. Mom! Marcus called me Mr. Wonka!"

"All right, go to bed," I tell him, patting his chest softly.

"Night, Marcus."

"Night, buddy,"

"Love you."

"Love you too."

❀❀❀

I tell my mom good night before heading back to my room. I take Danny's camera and look through the pictures of our trip. There are a whole bunch of photos of Charlie, my mom, Darma, Tío Ermenio, Sergio, María, Hilda, and Angela. There is one of Tío Pepe next to the pernil he roasted. There are several of the places we went on our road trip across the countryside. None of the fancy hotel. None of my dad.

I upload them onto the computer and put them in a file. I label the file and check my email. Danny has sent me a note. I open it. It says he spent all break getting kids to sign the petition to keep me in school. He tells me parents have signed it also. He says he's going to hold rallies at the school until they—dang, he uses big words—"exonerate me of all wrongdoing." Then he goes on to say what a punk Stephen is and that kids are starting to speak out in bigger numbers. He says Stephen is the one who should get expelled.

I appreciate the email. Danny is cool. But I don't want Stephen to get expelled. That's not going to do anything. A kid like Stephen is just scared. Scared of not being liked. Scared of things he doesn't understand. I don't hate him. I don't think he's ever going to use the R word again. Part of me wishes I hadn't punched him. I could've really hurt him. That's not cool. But then again, if I hadn't punched him, I may not have gone to PR.

I respond to Danny's email.

Thanks. I appreciate it, but I don't want
Stephen to get expelled. I just want to
go back to school and finish out the year.
Oh yeah, and thanks for the camera. I
attached some photos I took. They're of
family, mostly. I'll come by tomorrow to
return the camera. Thanks again, man.
Really.

—Marcus

I look at the file name attached to the email.

FAMILIA

I hit send and turn off the computer. I scan through
the pictures on Danny's camera one more time while
on my bed. I took over a thousand photos.

RETURN

TWENTY-TWO
QUESTIONS AND ANSWERS

On Monday, we all get up and have breakfast together. My mom makes scrambled eggs with bacon and cheese. Charlie is already dressed and ready to go to school. I worry about what Principal Jenkins is going to say. He already told my mom that the best thing for Charlie is a special school. The Academy for Exceptional Students. My brother is doing fine in public school. Still, though, I worry about him next year. My mom and I look at the flyer on the fridge. We're both thinking about it.

"It's expensive, Mom," I tell her. "Besides, Charlie deserves to be in a school like every other kid."

"He does, but I've been reading up on AES. They

really do have great schools all over. Even Miami, which is warm and beachside, just like PR."

"We're not going to move to Miami, Mom. Besides, we can't afford to put Charlie in AES. What about your job?"

"Well, look," she says. "I want changes, Marcus. I'm not saying we'll find them in Miami or New York or if we stay in Springfield. But I do know that I want things to be different."

I nod.

"So I'm going to talk to my supervisor about a promotion and I'm going to look at everything that is currently open across the airline. I want to explore all options."

"Great. Can we go to school now?"

"You're such a mood killer," she says, giving me a gentle shove.

"We're going to be late." I grab my things.

"No more sitting around, letting others tell us what we can or can't do. No more waiting." Mom takes a long sip of her coffee and stands. "Ready, boys?"

Charlie salutes her. "Mr. Wonka is ready!"

My mom starts singing. "Cuz I've got a golden ticket!"

Charlie joins in. "I've got a golden sun up in the sky!"

"Come on, Marcus, join in!"

"Nope."

"Come on!" Charlie grabs my arm. He tries to make

me dance, but I don't budge. There are a lot of changes going on. Me dancing isn't one of them.

My mom and Charlie keep it up all the way to the car.

I tell my mom to go ahead with Charlie. I'm going to meet up with Danny.

I head past the mechanic shop, the library, and across the street to where all the low rising buildings look the same. They aren't colorful like they are in Puerto Rico. I miss that. How can you miss a place where you only spent a few days?

I see Danny waiting on the corner outside his house. He stands up when he sees me coming.

"How many times do I have to tell you? You don't have to wait out here," I say.

"I know," he replies, "but it saves time."

This kid never learns. We walk down the street, and Danny asks me about my trip.

"Your pictures," he says. "They're really great."

We eventually meet up with the rest of the kids on the way to school. This isn't for money. I *want* to walk with them.

We get to campus and it's buzzing with students. Some are excited to catch up after a week off. Others in hoodies yawn as they drag themselves through the door. Danny says good-bye and zips inside the school. I walk up the stairs slowly. I can't lie—I'm anxious. What has everyone been saying over break about what happened with Stephen? What new names or rumors will I hear today?

I make eye contact with a kid chatting with a friend. She's one of my former Garbage Tax payers.

"Hi, Marcus," she says. I'm surprised she talks to me.

"Hi," I say.

"Had a good spring break?"

"Yeah," I say.

Her friend watches me. I shift my weight and put my hands in my pockets.

"I saw Charlie earlier," she says.

"He's so funny," the other kid offers.

"Yeah," I say.

"Only kid at school who knows everyone's name."

"I'm Jessica, by the way," the girl says. "This is Zach."

I nod. "Cool," I say, then I start heading inside.

"We signed the petition, you know?" she says.

I turn around.

"It wouldn't be middle school without big, bad Marcus Vega patrolling around." She smiles and winks.

She's joking. It's funny. I smile back.

"Thanks," I say.

"And not everyone around here feels like Stephen. Most of us don't."

Jessica gets up and Zach follows.

"See you around," she says. "Maybe the library?"

"No leaving trash around," I say, trying to make a joke.

She laughs. "Yes, sir, Mr. Assistant Principal."

I laugh. "Right. Now get out of here before I give you detention."

Jessica salutes, Zach gives me a high five, and then they turn to leave.

I walk down the hall in the other direction and watch as students zip by. Some say hello. Some smile. Some make eye contact. Not everyone, but more than usual.

A kid on his phone bumps into me.

He looks up and, without hesitating, offers me the phone.

"I don't do that anymore," I tell him. "Just keep it safe."

"Please save me from myself," he says. "I have an obsession with Clash of Clams. I can't stop playing it."

"My brother likes that game."

"I know," he says. "We play all the time during recess. We're in the same class."

"Really?"

"Yeah," he says, looking around like he's nervous or something. "He's my friend."

"That's cool. Be careful with the phone, okay? Just keep it in your locker."

"I will," he says.

"What's your name?" I ask him.

"Joey," he says. "My name is Joey."

Joey goes to his locker and takes out some books. He looks around, then finds a secure spot to put his phone. He closes his locker and gives me a thumbs-up.

I give him one back.

As I move farther down the hall, some kids move out of the way. At first I assume they're scurrying out of fear. But what if I have it wrong? Maybe they're just trying to get to class. I've thought of myself as a monster because that's what I was told I was. But I'm not. I'm just big. That's not a bad thing.

I walk straight to the office for my meeting with Principal Jenkins. I'm suddenly not sure how to feel. Even with the petition signed to keep me in school, I could still get expelled. I get to his office and hold my breath for a second before walking in.

❂❂❂

My mom and Stephen's mom go at it for a while. She keeps telling her that Stephen has a concerning history of tormenting kids and that he patrols the neighborhood preying on them after school. She asks to get a copy of the petition Danny created. When Stephen's mom tries to blame me again, my mom defends me. This post–Puerto Rico Mom is fierce. Who knew beautiful weather, old architecture, a gorgeous countryside, and exotic fruits and vegetables could do that to a person?

In the end, the suspension stays on my record. My mom tries to argue, but I tell her that I punched a kid.

"That's on me, Mom," I tell her. "There's no getting around it."

She knows I'm right.

Mr. Jenkins also reminds me that I have to stop collecting money for my various business ventures.

"No more profiting off my policies, Mr. Vega. Okay?"

I nod. I'm sure I can find another business venture outside of school. I'm not ready to totally give up Cookie Monster Cash.

Stephen doesn't get suspended, but he's on Mr. Jenkins's radar now. He won't be able to get away with anything.

And best of all, Charlie stays. He's even going to join the track team.

"I'm going to impress everyone with my cheetah speed!" he boasts.

My brother, the . . . Actually, I don't know what that is. It's something. He doesn't get it from me, that's for sure.

On my way to homeroom, I see Stephen walking to his locker. We eye each other.

I nod.

He does the same.

Nothing else needs to be said.

A few weeks after break, I'm still trying to figure some stuff out. If I'm not big, bad Marcus Vega—if I'm not using that to run businesses at school—who am I? Danny has been trying to help me find out. He organized an art night at school with my photographs from Puerto Rico. Seeing the portraits on display reminded me how much I missed everyone. My family.

A few parents and faculty members even bought some of the portraits. An eighth-grade girl named Sam said I "capture the soul of my subjects" in my photos. Whatever that means. It was nice of her to say, though.

I still walk the kids home every day. But like I said, I don't charge them anymore. I mostly just like the company, and I think they do too.

Sometimes I hang out with Danny or Charlie or just by myself, taking pictures. I like to visit the bodega next to the train and say hola to the lady at the counter. She speaks Spanish too fast, but I'm learning to understand her better. I take pictures of the mechanic shop on the way to school. I take pictures of the librarian pushing a cart of books down the stacks at the library. I take pictures of Danny, of my mom and Charlie, of my classmates, of the teachers walking in and out of classrooms, and of the large trees lining Cherry Hill. Everything that makes up this tiny town that's forty-five minutes from a big city and four hours away from an incredible island.

I think of the book Charlie picked up at the airport, *Proud to Be Boricua*. The author writes about the little singing frogs that I heard on Darma's farm. The coquí. He says, "Soy de aquí como el coquí." It literally means, "I am from here, like the coquí." From Puerto Rico. He belongs somewhere. I've been feeling the same way. I won't be croaking songs into the night like the tiny little frogs do. But it's nice to feel like I'm finally part of something that's way bigger than me.

AUTHOR'S NOTE

These pages show Puerto Rico as it was prior to the two catastrophic hurricanes that hit the island and the surrounding areas during the month of September in 2017. The severity of the crisis and the hardship that has befallen the people of Puerto Rico is tragic. When I struggle with words to describe the hurt I feel after the devastation, I think of a phrase I learned in PR. Pa'lante. It means go forward. Keep going forward. Though I could not have imagined such a tragedy at the time I wrote this book, I hope that now these pages honor the memory of the lives lost. There is still so much to be done to help those affected, but I look to the future with hope. Pa'lante seguimos.

ACKNOWLEDGMENTS

I am truly grateful to the people of Puerto Rico whom I've met in my travels. They showed me what it looks like to have spirit, strength, and pride in a place. To those of you traveling there: explore the island fully and its mountains, talk to the people, and listen to the coquí tell you its history.

To my editor, Joanna Cárdenas, who has a brilliant editorial eye and a gift for finding the true heart of a story. Thank you for everything you do to make my work shine. To Ken Wright and the entire Viking and Penguin Young Readers family for your support, hard work, and enthusiasm. A book's family is large and all of you care for it as your own. Gracias.

To my agent Jess Regel and the team at Foundry Literary + Media for always taking my calls. I know there are many. ☺

Thank you to Jessica Hermann-Quintero for her help with the German translations and Jorge Collazo for putting me in touch with many people in Puerto Rico.

To the countless individuals with special needs, especially those who I've come to know well at Our Pride Academy. These individuals are a testament to what is possible when the human heart is full of love, perseverance, and courage.

To Mami for listening and taking care of your family at every turn. Thank you, Papi, for showing me what it is to be a father. And for teaching me how to cook. That's really come in handy, Pops. For real. To my brothers, Guillo and Danny, and my extended family and friends: as always, thank you for your support and love. Los quiero mucho. Y gracias a Abuelo y Abuela for always protecting us.

To my daughter and son, who are hands down the best part of my day. And to Rebecca, who is the constant light in my world.

Turn the page for a sneak peek at Pablo's third novel: a tender story about a daughter and father finding their way back to each other in the face of their changing family and community.

CHAPTER ONE

I wasn't fast enough. Abuela appears behind me, already dressed with her makeup on, hair in a perfect bun. "Ven," she says, holding two brushes and a flatiron. She gestures for me to follow her into her room. I really wanted to get a few knots out of my hair before she got started.

She sits me down on the footstool facing her full-length mirror. As soon as my butt touches the seat, she hammers away with the hairbrush like she's some kind of black-smith hairstylist.

My head jerks as Abuela pulls. She takes a skinny comb with a long, pointy handle and splits my hair into sections with hair clips that look like chomping alligators. With one section in her hand, she takes the flatiron in the other. She feeds my hair into the iron and clamps down on the strands. Steam curls out like a dragon exhaling as the iron slides from the top of my head to my tips. Even though she's never burned me, I get nervous when Abuela gets close to my ears.

I don't have my mom's jet-black hair, but I have her curls. Or waves—my hair swooshes like a rolling tide. But after Abuela's done with it, it's as flat as a pancake. Today she straightens my hair out and puts it up into a ponytail.

"Pa'que se quede liso," she says. I guess she's worried that if I don't put my hair up, it will get wavy later. Abuela turns my head toward the window and keeps working.

There's something comforting about the way the sun enters the room through the curtains in the morning—it's like a *tap-tap-tapping* on the window, telling me it's time to get the day started. A cardinal chirps on the branch of our cedar tree. It flits around, and I'm jealous of the little bird for having so much energy in the morning. I lean over to draw the curtains open and let in more light.

"Quédate quieta, muchacha," Abuela says. "You're moving around too much."

"Aurelia," Mom says, popping into the room. "Déjala con su pelo risado."

Abuela stops tugging and looks back at Mom.

"She's going to go to school with her hair curly and out of control? She won't be able to focus," Abuela says.

"What?" my mom replies. "That's ridiculous."

"Well, what will people think? I'll tell you: that she doesn't have anybody to take care of her. Is that what you want?"

"That's what this is about," my mom says. "It's always about what other people think."

"It's important to put your best foot forward," Abuela says, continuing to brush out my ponytail.

"And I think her wavy hair is beautiful. It's her best foot, and I won't let you tell her otherwise." Mom winks while she scrunches her own hair.

"It's fine, Mom," I finally say.

It's not *really* fine—Abuela's daily hair rituals hurt, and I think my hair is like a lion's mane. And I love lions. But I'm not interested in Abuela and Mom getting into another argument over my hair.

Abuela finishes by putting a large blue bow on top of my head. I get up and move toward my mom, who is still standing at the door. She's wearing baggy sweatpants and a tank top and has her favorite fluffy argyle socks on. Her long, curly black hair falls along her shoulders like a waterfall in the dead of night.

I look back at my grandmother. She's wearing freshly

pressed pants and a blouse with circles and stars on it, her auburn hair perfectly in place without a loose strand. Her round rosy cheeks and thin lips are stained the color of an Arkansas Black apple, and she's wearing the same gold-and-pearl earrings she's worn since my abuelo died.

Between my mother and grandmother, I'm a blend of both. Short, head of wavy auburn hair, eyes large with dark yellow-green colors.

I don't have Mom's complexion. One that, as she once said, shows she is a "descendant of the Yoruba."

"Emilia viene de sangre española," Abuela replied. "She resembles *my* side of the family."

"She may have some Spanish ancestry," Mom said. "But she also has West African blood coursing through her veins. She needs to know *all* parts of her heritage, not just the European one—"

"Bueno," Abuela interrupted. "Remember, most of our family came from Spain. And some from Ireland. That's why your hair is that color, mi'ja."

"Si, pero you can't deny the orishas guide her spiritual journey as well," Mom said.

"Aye, muchacha," Abuela responded, clearly frustrated. "She's baptized Catholic."

"You baptized her Catholic, Aurelia," Mom said. Then she whispered to me loudly enough for Abuela to hear: "No matter what, nunca dudes lo que está in your mind and spirit, mi amor. That, and sea como sea, our Yoruba heritage teaches us to respect your elders."

Mom kissed my forehead.

I smiled. Abuela frowned.

"Come on," Mom says now. "Let's eat breakfast."

"Espérate." Abuela stops me before I head out.

She slathers her hands with gel and smooths the hair at the top of my forehead so it's flat against my scalp. I stare at myself in her full-length mirror as the plastering continues. My eyes follow Abuela's arm to the short cylindrical can she's digging into. Actually, it's pomade she's using. Not gel. Pomade is greasier and stays in my hair longer. It gives it a slick sheen, but honestly, I hate it because it takes forever to wash out. I don't say anything, though.

We walk downstairs, past the dining room that leads into the kitchen. Mom and I start our daily ritual of making café con leche, with a little slice of Cuban toast and melted butter, plus a large glass of my daily spinach-peanut-butter-banana-and-almond-milk smoothie.

"Doctor's recommendations!" Mom says, pouring the last of the smoothie into my glass.

"Why do I have to drink that horrible green monster *every* morning? It leaves specks of green in my teeth."

"It's not that bad! Here, take your fish oil pill."

"I hate that thing!"

"The doctor *did* say it's a natural way to help you concentrate."

Mom tries to add healthy foods into my diet *all* the time. She says it will help with my lack of focus. I think she's just trying to cut out sugar. Which I *love*.

As the coffee brews, the sweet and bitter smell wafts my way. Whoever figured out that those opposite tastes could blend together so perfectly in a coffee drink was a genius.

Mom puts her arm around me, and I lean into her shoulder.

"What's up, *Not*-Buttercup?" she jokes.

I perk up and smile.

I recently saw an old movie called *The Princess Bride* with Mom and Abuela. It's about this princess named Buttercup who falls in love with a guy named Westley. At one point in the movie, they're in a forest and these gigantic rats attack them. Westley falls to the ground while wrestling the rat, but Buttercup doesn't do anything. There's a humongous rat chewing on Westley's shoulder, and Buttercup doesn't even pick up a stick to bash it! She just stands there screaming for Westley to save her. It really annoyed me. Mom and Abuela eyed each other and said they never saw the movie that way.

Mom rubs my shoulder and gives it a squeeze.

"Ready for school?"

"No," I say, looking out the kitchen window, slurping up the last of my smoothie. Mom goes to the toaster and pulls out the warm bread and cuts it in half. Steam rises when she adds butter, and it melts instantly. She moves the knife like she's conducting an orchestra across each slice.

My mouth feels dry, but it's not because I'm thirsty.

"Do you have to leave?" I ask her.

"Yes, baby girl. The conference starts tomorrow."

"But it's, like, a thirty-hour time difference, Mom."

"It's San Francisco, mi amor. Not China. And it's only a little more than a week. Who knows? Something exciting could come of it."

"Like what?" I ask, moving over to help her. I grab a paper towel and start wiping the loose crumbs off the counter.

"We'll see! Anyway, Dad is coming home tonight," she tells me. "You'll get some one-on-one time with him for a few days!"

"And apparently he's okay with your mother leaving even though he's been gone for eight months," Abuela says, stern at the kitchen door. It doesn't seem to faze Mom at all. She's used to what she calls Abuela's "puyas"—side comments meant to get under her skin. Abuela throws shade like a chameleon changes colors.

Mom rubs my forearm and squeezes my hand a little. "Bueno, Aurelia, luckily my husband and I have communicated, and fortunately for both of us, we understand that our jobs may require a certain amount of travel on occasion. As I'm sure you've experienced over the years with his deployments."

Abuela huffs and leaves the kitchen. Mom exhales slowly.

"How do you not get flustered by her, Mom?"

"Patience, mi amor," Mom says. "The older you get, the more important patience becomes."

I glance over at my backpack and think about all the classes I have and how Mom is always there to help organize my work and how I can't let Abuela help me because she won't understand and suddenly I feel the vibrating in my head that happens sometimes when I get nervous. It's like a whole bunch of little bees buzzing around and it's hard to concentrate.

"Mom, who's going to help me with my homework when you're gone?"

"Dad will!"

The calendar Mom and I go over every Monday morning to help me organize the week sits in front of me. Friday is circled with two little stars and a question mark next to it.

"Oh, Mom! Clarissa is having a party on Friday. Can I go?"

"It's Monday, Emilia. And that's not really relevant to our discussion, is it?"

"So?"

"Well, we're talking about your dad coming home tonight and since it's Monday, I think planning for your *school* week is the priority, don't you think?"

"Mom, please don't start that priority–organizational thinking thing again. I know it's Monday."

"Okay, but you have a math—"

"I know! Geez." I take a breath and exhale. Patience . . .
Right.

"Don't make that face," she says.

"What face?"

"The one that looks like you ate day-old bacalao."

Mom drops her upper lip and her eyes sag a little.

"I hate salted cod," I tell her.

"Oye, your ancestors are probably rolling in their graves."

I drop my head onto my mom's shoulder again. When
I lift it, she hands me her mug. "Bueno, at least you like
café con leche."

I take a sip, and everything comes into focus. There is
nothing like café con leche. Nothing.

"C'mon, mi amor. Let's hang out a little before the bus
gets here," she says.

Mom pats my back and heads to the dining room, carrying the café con leche. I follow her with the buttery Cuban
toast and sit at the dining table, where we've done homework together hundreds of times. Probably thousands.
Maybe millions. Abuela moves past us to the kitchen.

"Should we get him balloons or a sign or something?"
I ask.

"No, you know he doesn't like a big welcome like that,"

Mom says. "Be there with a hug and tell him you're glad he's home."

"Well, I *am* glad he's home. I just wish you were going to be home too."

"I know, baby. But this is going to be good. Trust me."

"Yeah, yeah," I say, swinging my feet and munching on toast and talking about the week ahead. She likes to go over my agenda for the week, but it's kind of annoying because sometimes that's all she talks about.

"So, you got it?"

"Hmm?"

"Your stuff for the week, sweetheart," she says. "Math test Thursday. You have a vocabulary test Friday. What do you have for social studies?"

"Oh, Clarissa's party! I can go, right?"

"Emilia," Mom says, using my name like a sharp-edged sword to make her point. "I need to be able to go on this trip knowing you're ready for the week."

"Yes, Mom, you've told me, like, a hundred times!"

"And social studies?"

"What about it?"

"What do you have for Mr. Richt's class this week?"

"I don't know, something. Maybe a test."

"Maybe? Do I have to call?"

"No, Mami! Please, can we just talk about something else?"

She lets out a sigh. "Okay, mi amor. What do you want to talk about?"

I ask her about her trip, where she's going to present this cool new translation app she designed.

"Are you going to speak in front of a ton of people?"

"I hope not!" she says. "I hate speaking in front of people."

"But you have to talk about it."

"Oh, I have no problem talking one-on-one," she says. "I just hate talking in front of big crowds. Me da pánico."

"You won't panic, Mom," I tell her. "It's going to be awesome."

"I hope so. It'll be a game changer."

I hear the bus rounding the corner, rumbling like a grumpy yellow rhino that hasn't had coffee yet. Would a rhino drink café con leche? Probably. I wish I had a remote control that could pause the bus for a moment longer.

"It's time to go, mi amor." Mom gets up and hugs me.

"I'm going to miss you," I tell her. Her curls wrap around

my shoulders like a dark rain cloud that blocks out the sun and cools the sky.

"I'll call when I land," she says, kissing my forehead. "And you call me for *anything*. Okay?"

"I will," I say, getting up and heading to the door.

Abuela comes back into the dining room and hands me a waffle wrapped in a napkin. The syrup drips onto the napkin and the paper sticks to the waffle. I try to peel it off, but the syrup has already glued it in place.

"Tienes que desayunar más," Abuela says.

"Ya comí, Abuela," I reply, showing her my mostly eaten toast.

She shakes her head. "Pero that tiny piece of bread and that green milkshake aren't enough," she says. "You have to have a full stomach at school, Emilia Rosa."

Mom steps in and takes the waffle out of my hand.

"Aurelia," Mom says. "We talked about this, remember? Her doctor suggested eliminating sugar to see what effect it has on her inattentiveness."

"And the café con leche you gave her this morning? That has sugar."

"It has almond milk and a tiny bit of agave in it."

Abuela shakes her head, then lets out a humph before taking the waffle from my mom. "Whoever heard of café con leche with *agave*?" she mutters loudly enough for both of us to hear.

Mom steps around her to hug me one more time. "Don't let her get to you," she whispers. Abuela frowns. Mom kisses me on the nose and playfully pats my side. "Love you, baby."

"Love you too, Mom," I say, heading outside. "Have a good trip."

"Thanks, mi amor."

"Bye, Abuela," I say, quickly pecking her on the cheek and grabbing my backpack.

"Have a good day, mi'ja," she responds.

The bus is already in front of our house when I step outside. Its doors swing open, and I turn back to look at Mom one more time.

Abuela calls out and rushes to the bus before I get on. She holds my head, tucks a few loose strands of hair behind my ears, and tightens my bow.

"Perfect," she says.

I think about taking a deep breath, but I just get on the bus.

It feels like my whole life is changing. Like everything that's normal is becoming the opposite. We've been like this for so long—me, Mom, and Abuela. Now that Mom is leaving and Dad is coming home—with Abuela probably in charge—I'm not sure what to expect.

A Discussion Guide to

PABLO CARTAYA

THE EPIC FAIL OF
ARTURO ZAMORA

MARCUS VEGA
DOESN'T SPEAK SPANISH

EACH TINY SPARK

A 2018 PURA BELPRÉ AUTHOR HONOR BOOK
Save the restaurant. Save the town. Get the girl. Make Abuela proud. Can thirteen-year-old Arturo Zamora do it all, or is he in for a BIG, EPIC FAIL?

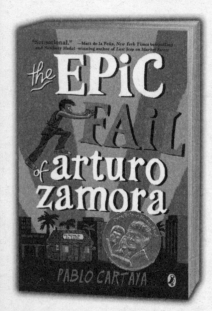

For Arturo, summertime in Miami means playing basketball until dark, sipping mango smoothies, and keeping cool under banyan trees. And maybe a few shifts as junior lunchtime dishwasher at Abuela's restaurant. Maybe. But this summer also includes Carmen, a poetry enthusiast who moves into Arturo's apartment complex and turns his stomach into a deep fryer. He almost doesn't notice the smarmy land developer who rolls into town and threatens to change it. Arturo refuses to let his family and community go down without a fight, and as he schemes with Carmen, Arturo discovers the power of poetry and protest through untold family stories and the work of José Martí.

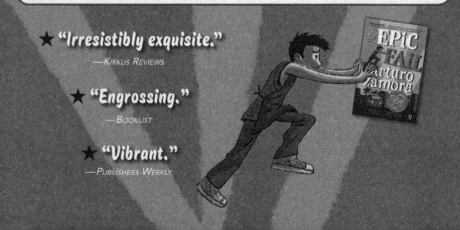

★ "Irresistibly exquisite."
—KIRKUS REVIEWS

★ "Engrossing."
—BOOKLIST

★ "Vibrant."
—PUBLISHERS WEEKLY

DISCUSSION QUESTIONS

1. This novel begins with Arturo's "Note to Self." What is the effect of the book beginning here?

2. Why is food so important to Arturo and his family?

3. Look at Chapter 4, "Ice Scream: a Dialogue." This chapter is very different from the rest of the novel. Why did the author choose to make this almost like a play with dialogue and stage directions?

4. Who was José Martí? Why is he so important for this book?

5. Carmen's protest sign reads "FAMILY IS COMMUNITY—COMMUNITY IS FAMILY." What does this mean?

6. After Arturo is upset because he feels like he failed, he takes a moment to directly address the reader of his book. "Dear reader, I told you not to be fooled by high expectations." Why do you think he talks directly to the reader? Did you feel like he was talking to you? Explain.

7. What are Arturo's epic fails? How do they impact him, and those around him, throughout the story?

8. Is Wilfrido Pipo evil? Why or why not?

9. Why does Arturo decide to use a poem to address the neighborhood?

EXTENSION ACTIVITIES

Arturo, Carmen, and Arturo's family protest Pipo's proposed plan. While their involvement is on a large scale, think of something that's happening in your own community and create a protest sign to advocate for yourself, your class, your school, or whoever! On the back of the sign, explain the history of the situation and propose an idea for how to fix it. (CCSS.ELA-LITERACY.WHST.6-8.1, CCSS.ELA LITERACY.WHST.6-8.2)

Arturo's abuelo leaves him letters. Write a letter to your own future relatives—tell about a time when you made a difference in the world and give your future relative wisdom about how they could be a changemaker. (CCSS.ELA-LITERACY.W.6.3)

One boy's search for his father leads him to Puerto Rico, in this moving middle-grade novel.

Marcus Vega is six feet tall, 180 pounds, and the owner of a premature mustache. When you look like this and you're only in the eighth grade, you're both a threat and a target.

After a fight at school leaves Marcus facing suspension, Marcus's mom decides it's time for a change of environment. She takes Marcus and his younger brother to Puerto Rico to spend a week with relatives they don't remember or have never met. But Marcus can't focus knowing that his father—who walked out of their lives ten years ago—is somewhere on the island.

Marcus's journey takes him all over Puerto Rico. He doesn't know if he'll ever find his father, but what he ultimately discovers changes his life. And he even learns a bit of Spanish along the way.

★ **"Excellent."**

★ **"An ideal read for boys or reluctant readers."**

DISCUSSION QUESTIONS

1. When we are introduced to Marcus, he's described as "the Mastodon of Montgomery Middle, the Springfield Skyscraper, the Moving Mountain, the Terrible Tower," but his actions and care for his brother contradict these images of him as a big monster. How would you describe Marcus instead?

2. Why does Principal Jenkins suggest Charlie attend another school?

3. Marcus's businesses help enforce school rules. Is it wrong that he's making money by doing this? Explain.

4. Do you think Danny's petition to keep Marcus in school was useful? Why did Danny start this petition?

5. Why does Marcus's mother eventually decide that the family should go to Puerto Rico?

6. The book is called *Marcus Vega Doesn't Speak Spanish*, and throughout the novel Marcus himself admits that he doesn't know the language. Is this true? Do you think Marcus doesn't know Spanish? Explain.

7. How do you feel about the fact that much of the Spanish dialogue isn't translated? Why might the author have chosen to not include an English translation or glossary?

8. Marcus gets angry a few times during this book—he punches Stephen, and later he also punches Sergio's truck. What could he do to better channel his emotions?

9. What does Charlie mean when he tells his father, "You broke the rules!" after he tries to explain his absence to Marcus?

10. Marcus observes that Puerto Rico changed his mom: "This post–Puerto Rico Mom is fierce. Who knew beautiful weather, old architecture, a gorgeous countryside, and exotic fruits and vegetables could do that to a person?" Do you think Puerto Rico changed Marcus and Charlie, too? If so, how?

EXTENSION ACTIVITIES

In the Author's Note at the end of the book, Pablo Cartaya explains that this book represents a Puerto Rico before it was devastated by hurricanes in 2017. Knowing that Puerto Rico's landscape was so changed by these events, do some research on Puerto Rico before and after the hurricanes and write a compare and contrast report explaining the significant changes to the island after these events. (CCSS.ELA-LITERACY.RST.6-8.1, CCSS.ELA-LITERACY.W.6.7, CCSS.ELA-LITERACY.RI.5.6)

Keeping in mind the travel guides Charlie gets in the airport for Puerto Rico, create your own travel guide for the island. Your guide should incorporate images, text, and other elements to encourage travelers to visit Puerto Rico. (CCSS.ELA-LITERACY.WHST.6-8.4, CCSS.ELA-LITERACY.WHST.6-8.6)

A sparkling middle grade novel about a daughter and father finding their way back to each other in the face of their changing family and community.

Emilia Torres has a wandering mind. It's hard for her to follow along at school, and sometimes she forgets to do what her mom or abuela asks. But she remembers what matters: a time when her family was whole and home made sense. When Dad returns from deployment, Emilia expects that her life will get back to normal. Instead, it unravels.

Dad shuts himself in the back stall of their family's auto shop to work on an old car. Emilia peeks in on him daily, mesmerized by his welder. One day, Dad calls Emilia over. Then he teaches her how to weld. And over time, flickers of her old dad reappear.

But as Emilia finds a way to repair the relationship with her father at home, her community ruptures, with some of her classmates, like her best friend, Gus, at the center of the conflict.

DISCUSSION QUESTIONS

1. Why does Emilia record videos to send to her father when he is deployed?

2. Emilia and her family drink café con leche, Cuban coffee. Her mother says that the smell of it is "'the sweet aroma of our island [Cuba] and our ancestors.'" What does that mean?

3. Why does Emilia choose to begin her tour at the Latino food store?

4. When Emilia discovers that the Olympic stadium was built by immigrants who then risked deportation, she wonders about the fate of her family members who are immigrants. She thinks: "Who makes the rules about who gets to stay somewhere and who has to leave?" This is a big question. Should someone have the power to dictate where others live? If they stay or go?

5. Why do you think many students in Emilia's class don't know about the history of Park View and Merryville?

6. Why does Gus forgive Emilia for standing him up at Clarissa's party?

7. Why does Mr. Richt cancel the travel brochure project?

8. Eventually, Emilia Rosa insists that Clarissa call her by her real name, instead of "Emi Rose." Why is it so important that Emilia Rosa be called by her real, full name?

9. Describe Emilia's relationships with her family (mother, father, and grandmother). Why would she be okay with her mother taking the job in San Fransisco when her family is so rarely all together?

10. Emilia's father makes her a video at the end of the book. How does Emilia react to this video?

EXTENSION ACTIVITIES

Emilia and Gus's video makes a big impact on their school, and Mr. Richt even hopes to share it with the community. In keeping with this moment in the text, make a video, like Emilia and Gus, about something going on at your school. The videos should include interviews and other footage relevant to the topic. (CCSS.ELA-LITERACY.RH.6-8.7)

So many of Pablo Cartaya's books seek to understand familial connections, but they also highlight the families that we make for ourselves that often transcend biological relations. Keeping this in mind, create family trees (both biological and chosen), doing research on your family archives to construct relations and see connections. These projects should be creative and should be accompanied by a brief, reflective writing where you explain your creative processes. (CCSS.ELA-LITERACY.WHST.6-8.10, CCSS.ELA-LITERACY.W.5.5, CCSS.ELA-LITERACY.W.5.7)

About
PABLO CARTAYA

Pablo Cartaya is an award-winning author, speaker, actor, and educator. In 2018, he received a Pura Belpré Author Honor for his middle grade novel *The Epic Fail of Arturo Zamora*. His second novel, *Marcus Vega Doesn't Speak Spanish*, is available now. His third novel, *Each Tiny Spark*, publishes in 2019. Learn more about Pablo at pablocartaya.com and follow him on Twitter @phcartaya.

PenguinClassroom.com

 PenguinClassroom   **@PenguinClass**   **PenguinClassroom**

This guide was written by Cristina Rhodes. Cristina is an incoming assistant professor of ethnic literature. Her research explores Latinx youth identities and activism in children's literature.